PASSAGE UP THE MEKONG

RICK AND ROSE SINCLAIR ADVENTURE #4

RUSSELL JAMES

SEVERED**PRESS**

PASSAGE UP THE MEKONG

Copyright © 2025 by Russell James

WWW.SEVEREDPRESS.COM

ISBN: 978-1-923165-55-7

Other books by Russell James

Rick and Rose Sinclair Adventures
Quest for the Queen's Temple
Voyage to Blackbeard's Island
Quest for the City of Gold

Grant Coleman Adventures
Cavern of the Damned
Monsters in the Clouds
Curse of the Viper King
Forest of Fire
Mammoth Island
Atoll X
Desolation Canyon

Ranger Kathy West National Park Adventures
Claws
Dragons of Kilauea
Ravens of Yellowstone

Dedication

For Christy,
Who's always up for an adventure.

PROLOGUE

In the Cambodian jungle along the Mekong River
1938

Abbott Dara sat deep in contemplation. Suddenly, he wasn't.

His eyes snapped wide open. Every sense went to high alert. His pulse rate soared. Dara rose from his cross-legged seating position. Joints creaked and muscles moaned as he did. He leaned against the mildewed stone wall for support.

Dara stood in the portico of the main temple of the crumbling Buddhist monastery. He tightened the abbot's purple sash that bound his saffron-colored robe at his waist. He listened for whatever sound had jerked him so abruptly and completely out of his meditation.

He heard nothing special. Insects and birds common to the Cambodian jungle sang the harmony of the usual background noise. Two monks nearby held a subdued conversation while they worked a garden plot. Off to his left, a muted gong sounded, starting a group prayer among other monks. There seemed to be nothing amiss here.

But Dara knew there was.

He could sense a shift in the fabric of the Earth. It was as if a frayed thread had just broken, and the unraveling of the whole cloth was now inevitable. Would his monks be ready when that cataclysm came? He had to hope so.

Karma was the great leveler, adding woe to those who took advantage of others and bestowing blessings on those forced into despair. But karma did not work like a butter knife, constantly leveling the spread atop a piece of toast. Often it reacted more like the ocean at the beach, receding to leave crabs and seaweed parched and dying, before returning in a massive wave to set the seashore back in balance.

Dara sensed the beginning of that time of death and misery, a moment he and his monks had deeply dreaded and knew was long overdue. He wondered if they, and he in his eighth decade of life, would survive both the agony of karma's withdrawal and the fury of it setting things right again.

CHAPTER ONE

Savannah, Georgia

As far as Rick was concerned, being stuck in the Treasure Hunters Antiques shop was one step short of a prison sentence.

It wasn't the shop that was the problem. He and his wife had owned and operated it for years. Tucked into one of the downtown streets in Savannah, Georgia, it had made enough money to get them through the worst of what people had started calling the Great Depression. His problem was being unable to go much of anywhere else.

The doctor he'd seen when they returned to Savannah from their adventure in the wilds of Mexico had done a fine job setting his broken leg. He'd been lucky that it had been a hairline fracture. But the plaster cast and crutches meant he wasn't driving, in fact not even walking, far from the store. He and Rose lived in the apartment over the shop, so "going home" at the end of the day wasn't liberating at all. Rose had been great about carrying the full load while he was healing, but he hated feeling trapped.

Worse, he hated feeling useless. Right now, Rose was out delivering part of an estate they'd sold, and they'd had to hire some help to load and unload the stuff from the truck. That wasn't financially sustainable, especially since the sale of the helmet they'd brought back from the discovered Aztec temple had barely covered the cost of the Mexico trip. In addition, it didn't do anything for his ego to watch someone do the work he was supposed to do. And the work he was doing instead, minding the store, could have been done by a shop girl.

3

Standing behind the counter would have been murder on his leg, so he'd taken one of the rocking chairs for sale, moved it beside the register, and set an ottoman in front of it. Settled into this seat, he could see anyone entering the shop and into most of the aisles of goods.

A bell rang and announced the opening of the front door. In stepped Matty Mahoney. Rick sighed and stood up.

Rose's predisposition was to dislike on sight most of Rick's friends, and Matty was one of the reasons why. Some of Rick's business actions walked a fine line between honest and dishonest. Matty's kind of deal usually crashed through that line without braking. The weasel-like little man wore a tattered fedora and a workingman's shirt and trousers, which was ironic since Rick was sure the man hadn't worked a straight job since doing his teenage streetcorner newspaper sales. Matty carried a stained, brown paper bag in one hand.

Matty turned around and cast furtive glances up and down the street through the front window. He had the look of a man holding a pair of threes with his life savings already thrown in the pot. Apparently satisfied that he'd entered the shop unobserved, he turned to see Rick. Matty assumed an unconvincing smile.

"Ricky, old pal," he said. "How's tricks?"

"Not bad. Long time, no see, Matty."

"Well, you know me. Always a new deal, always on the move."

"Always a step ahead of the police," Rick said.

"Oh, ha ha. Such a kidder, Ricky, really. But I've got something for you, something one of your high roller customers would like."

Matty put the paper bag on the counter. He reached in and pulled out something secured in a white silk bag. Matty untied the bag and slid out a larger than life-sized, stone-sculpted human hand. Rick raised an eyebrow. The stone looked like jade.

"May I?" Rick said.

"Sure, sure. That's solid jade there, a hundred percent."

Rick picked up the hand. The heft and the coldness confirmed it was solid stone. He turned the piece under the light. The polished surface was perfectly smooth and the seams between stones nearly imperceptible. This piece was the real deal.

"What's a nice girl like you," Rick said to the jade hand, "doing with a mug like this guy?"

"Hey, watch it, Ricky. This is on the up-and-up, totally legit. I knew a guy who knew a guy and I got it cheap. Rich folks are getting desperate in this Depression, you know?"

Rick knew they were. He'd seen them come into the shop ready to dump valuable heirlooms to make ends meet. "You can leave it here on consignment. I'll pay you when it sells."

Matty's face fell. "Oh, Ricky, that ain't no good. I'm looking for cash now. I got some pressing bills, you know?"

Given Matty's history, Rick guessed Matty's bill collectors were the kind who charged high interest and broke bones for non-payment.

"What do you say you buy it, huh?" Matty said.

"What do you want for it?"

Matty gave him a price. It was as much money as Rick and Rose had in their savings account. But it was also a third of what this piece was worth, even just for the weight of the jade.

"This thing isn't cursed, is it?" Rick said with a smile.

Fear filled Matty's face. "What? No! Nothing like that. C'mon, Ricky. What do you say? Help a fellow out in a jam?"

Rick rubbed a finger against the hand's glossy finish. This was exactly the kind of thing he was always telling Rose they should buy, something with a low-end price that was good for a high-end sale. Things might get financially tight for a while, but when this sold, they'd be on Easy Street for sure.

Rick noticed something printed on the silk bag. He flipped it over and revealed a stitched logo of a sword and a shield. Beneath it was stitched GRAND DUCHY MUSEUM.

"Oh, that," Matty said. "I had that bag lying around. Thought it would keep the jade from being scratched."

Rick looked sideways at Matty. Kids told better lies. But Rick had handled items with questionable provenance before. Just not items with this much of a potential payday attached to them.

"You have a deal," Rick said. "I'll cut you a check."

Matty looked so relieved, Rick was afraid the guy was going to hug and kiss him. "That's my boy. I tell everyone, Rick's the one who'll give you a fair shake. Trust me, you won't regret this."

Rick had been holding the hand for a few moments. It still felt unnaturally cold. Second thoughts about this purchase popped into his head. He pushed them away. He needed to trust his gut on this one. Matty was right. He wouldn't regret it.

Once he'd explained it to Rose, that is.

CHAPTER TWO

It was almost five PM when Rose walked in the back door. Her red hair was a bit askew and her normally porcelain-white skin was a little flushed. The sight of her in any condition still made Rick's heart race. Rick went to her to give her a kiss.

She held up her hands. "Whoa. I'm too much of a mess. It was hot as hell and that delivery was serious work."

"But we paid those two freshmen from Martyn University to do the work."

"Well, I couldn't just stand there and watch, like some helpless female."

Rick knew that had been likely to happen. His wife was always dead-set on pulling her own weight in every situation. Nothing infuriated her faster than some man belittling her capabilities because she was female.

"I'll be out of this cast the day after tomorrow," Rick said, "and ready to resume my manly endeavors."

Rose gave him a sideways look. "What did you do?"

"What do you mean?"

"You have that stupid look on your face you always get when you've done something you know I'll be mad about."

Rick wasn't ready to tell her about the jade hand yet, not until he knew more about it. "Rosie, I was here limping around the shop the whole time. What could I do?"

"Little would surprise me there."

"I'm hurt by your accusatory tone. You should trust your husband a little more."

Her eyes bored into his. He flashed a sheepish grin.

"Okay," Rose sighed. "Sorry. A half-dozen things went wrong today and I guess I was primed for one more disaster once I got home."

"Don't give up hope. You haven't seen the kitchen yet. I bumped a glass off the counter and it shattered." He knocked on his cast with his fist. "No way I could bend down and use a dustpan."

"I can deal with that just fine. C'mon, I'll help you up the stairs to the apartment."

"I'll be up in a bit. Humphrey's dropping by."

"Humphrey?"

Humphrey Custis was a former Great War fighter ace turned Depression pilot-of-all-trades, including those of dubious legality. He wasn't too high on Rose's acceptability list either.

"You should be thrilled," Rick said. "He's paying me back five dollars he borrowed."

"I'll bet he tries to borrow ten before he heads back out the door."

Rose headed upstairs. A few minutes later, Humphrey came in the front door. His faded overalls and frayed shirt collar made him look like a down-on-his-luck farmer. His ample belly stretched the overalls' bib to its limit. The only thing that hinted he was a professional pilot was the spiffy-looking, khaki peaked military cap on his head.

"Humphrey, old chum. Looks like you've finally gotten yourself a new hat."

Humphrey grinned. "Sure enough. Army surplus, just like the one I had in the Great War. Fits real nice, too."

Rick poked his belly. "Which is more than we can say for your old uniform."

"Now that was a right unkind comment, Rick. So, what did you want to show me?"

Rick waved his hands in front of Humphrey's face. "Shhh! Rose is upstairs."

"Don't she know I'm here?"

"Sure, but she doesn't know about what I'm going to show you. Follow me."

Rick led Humphrey behind the counter. He took out a brown paper bundle tied with twine. Rick pulled the knot free, unrolled the paper, and revealed the jade hand.

Humphrey caught his breath. He set his hat on the counter with the kind of reverence reserved for a royal crown, and then bent over the jade for a closer look. "Whoa, Rick. That there's prettier than a picture postcard. Where'd you get it?"

"From Matty Mahoney."

"So, it's stolen."

"Hey, you're jumping to a conclusion. We don't know that."

"Matty's fingers are stickier than a bear's paws at a beehive."

"The point here is that since you've travelled all over, I was wondering if you might have ever seen anything like it."

Humphrey picked up the hand and turned it this way and that in the light. "Damn fine workmanship, I'll tell you that. And most of the good jade like this comes out of the French colonies in southeast Asia."

Rick clenched a fist in victory. "I knew it was worth something big."

"Big trouble," Rose said from behind them.

Rick whirled around. "Rosie! I thought you were making dinner."

"No, I knew you were up to something as soon as you told me Humphrey was coming over to pay you back a loan. Like that would ever happen."

Humphrey gave Rick an admonishing look. "You told her that, Rick? Even I know that ain't believable."

"Where did you get that hand?" Rose said.

"Matty."

"So, it's stolen?"

"See, Rick?" Humphrey said. "It ain't jumping to conclusions if everyone does it."

"It isn't stolen," Rick said. "The point is, we have honest possession of it now, and we can pass that honest possession to someone else at a profit."

"How much did you pay for this future exhibit at our felony theft trial?" Rose said.

"Far less than what it's worth."

"Which is how much?"

"Slightly less than we have in our savings account."

Rose's face turned red. "What? How could you do that?"

"Because this is a sure thing. We'll turn this around in a day or two, tops. We know plenty of people who collect Southeast Asian art."

"You didn't even know this was Southeast Asian art until the flyboy here told you."

"I had a gut feeling this would be a big score."

"Every time you have a gut feeling," Rose said, "I end up with ulcers. How is that?"

"Rose," Humphrey said. "I do know a Chinese fella does a lot of exporting from there since the Japanese invaded China. I know for sure he'd be interested."

"See," Rick said. "It's as good as sold."

"It had better be," Rose said. "Otherwise, we're going to have some unpaid bills."

"Trust me," Rick said.

Rose rolled her eyes. "Those are the least reassuring words you've ever spoken."

CHAPTER THREE

Rose slammed the plates down on the kitchen table so hard that she almost broke them.

She loved her husband. Her heart still raced every time he cracked that charming Errol Flynn-like smile. They had been on some adventures together and he'd risked his life numerous times to save hers. His almost-healed broken leg was proof of that. She could stack him up against any number of her friends' husbands and he would come out on top.

But Rick was a gambler, and not just when playing cards. The opportunity for the big payday attracted him like candy did children. He'd made some seriously boneheaded purchases without letting her know about the deal. She'd nearly punched him the time he brought home a ragged taxidermized polar bear. Most of his "finds" flopped, but a few had turned a profit. And like all gamblers, Rick remembered the wins and the losses became hazy memories.

But she could tell that this jade hand was going to be a bigger headache than all his other questionable purchases. Matty Mahoney was as trustworthy as a snake and would not only sell you a stolen item, he'd then turn you in for owning it if a reward was offered. And that jade hand was certainly stolen. Matty did not travel in the kind of circles where sculptures like that came up for sale.

And adding insult to injury, Rick had told Humphrey about it before he'd told her. Humphrey wasn't as bad an influence as Matty, but he was a close second. He'd been a lot of help on their adventures, but she was sure he was always one smuggling trip away from ending up in a prison.

Rose was certain no good would come of this purchase. If their life savings hadn't been wrapped up in the jade hand, she would have tossed the thing in the trash and been done with it.

She heard the step-bump footfall pattern of Rick and his leg cast climbing the steps up to their apartment. He was going to get an extra helping of "what-were-you-thinking" along with his potatoes tonight.

Rick stepped into the kitchen. Humphrey stood behind him. Rose started to tell Rick after his stupid purchase he was lucky there was dinner for two, let alone adding a plate for Humphrey.

"I thought I'd help Rick up the stairs." Humphrey poked Rick in the back and moved him one step forward. "And help him say something else."

"Rosie," Rick said. "I really should have got you involved in buying the jade hand. I got excited and just jumped at the chance for something special."

"That tends to be what you do."

Rick smiled. "That's how I married you and that worked out great."

"You do not want to put that up for a vote right now."

"And Humphrey promised to help me line up that buyer first thing in the morning," Rick said.

"As soon as the cock crows," Humphrey said, "I'm starting the phone calls."

Rose felt her heart soften. As always with Rick, a little honest contrition went a long way. "Okay, but so help me, if we lose money on this, I'll toss you down those stairs and break your other leg."

From downstairs came the crash of splintering wood. Rose caught her breath.

"What was that?" she said.

"Nothing good," Rick said.

Humphrey headed back down the stairs. Rick followed him at a much slower one-step-at-a-time pace.

Rose was right behind him. Flush with a combination of impatience and worry, she had to restrain herself from pushing him aside.

At the bottom of the steps, the scene in the shop made Rose furious. The front door yawned open, the lockset and door jamb smashed. The chair behind the counter lay on its side. The good news was that no one was there, and the cash register was still closed.

"Oh no." Rick hobbled back behind the counter and looked underneath it. "The hand is gone."

"You left it out under the counter?" Rose said.

Outside an engine roared to life. Humphrey and Rose ran to the front window. A black Lincoln sedan squealed the tires as it accelerated away from the shop.

Rose pushed Humphrey toward his car parked at the curb. "What are you waiting for? Follow them!"

Humphrey dashed for his car. Rick stepped past Rose. "We'll get them," he said.

Rose blocked his way with her arm. "No way, Hopalong. You'll just slow Humphrey down, and he's not that swift to begin with."

Rick relented and stepped back. "I don't get how anyone could even know it was here."

"Clearly, whoever it was stolen from followed Matty here, watched through the window while you and Humphrey ogled it, and then grabbed it as soon as you made your way upstairs."

"Humphrey will get it back."

"You'd better hope he does or we'll have to start living out of the back of our Model A truck."

***

Humphrey jumped into his car and slammed the door. The car rattled and the door lock didn't catch. He slammed it again and rust tinkled down from the roof and into his hair. He realized he'd left his new hat behind and cursed himself.

His 1925 Packard coupe looked like hell. The tall styling and open fenders were hopelessly outdated and the body sported as much rust as paint. But the big Packard Straight 8 under the hood still purred like a kitten at idle and then roared like a lion when he hit the accelerator. A car with an underwhelming appearance and overwhelming performance was perfect for the kind of work Humphrey did.

Humphrey hit the starter and the car rumbled to life with a puff of black smoke. He dropped the clutch and sped off in the direction the Lincoln had gone. The Savannah streets were near empty and he hoped the thief hadn't gotten too large a lead on him. The sun was almost down and it was getting dusky.

He caught sight of a big black car further down the road. Humphrey prayed that was the one. As he closed on it, he saw it was slowing down. Seemed like the thief had relaxed, thinking he'd gotten away scot-free. All the better for Humphrey.

The Lincoln cruised through Savannah until it got to the river. There it turned left for the main shipping docks. Humphrey doused his lights and followed at a discrete distance.

A mile or so down the road, the Lincoln stopped at the gate to one of the dock areas. A high fence topped with barbed wire encircled several acres of riverfront. Inside the perimeter stood a number of large warehouses and a wide shipping dock. After the Lincoln's driver had a brief exchange with the guard, the guard opened the gate and let them pass.

Humphrey was certain he would not be extended the same courtesy. But he wouldn't need it. This wasn't the first time he'd visited this particular dock without an invitation.

He spun the car around and turned on the lights. A minute later he spotted a familiar rutted road to the left. He killed the lights again and followed it along the property's chain link fence. The fence went all the way down to the river, but Humphrey stopped the car just short of the riverbank. The area inside the fence was a warren of empty crates and containers waiting to be reused for some outbound cargo. The warehouse area had looked deserted, but in case any workers were there, the crates would keep him hidden from their view.

"Now it was right here somewheres," he muttered. "Or at least a bunch of years ago it was."

The lights from the river dock gave the fence a bit of illumination. They reflected better off the intimidating roll of barbed wire running along the top. Humphrey picked up a pair of gloves from the floorboards, eased out of the car, and made his way to a familiar support pole. Here a number of the links in the fence had been slightly widened in an alternating pattern on either side of the pole. From a distance it wasn't noticeable, but they made for the perfect hand and footholds to scale the fence.

Humphrey tucked a toe into one opening, grabbed another with his hand, and climbed. His stomach bumped against the metal with each movement, something he didn't remember happening the last time he'd scaled it.

At the top of the fence, two strands of barbed wire overlapped, but were not tied together. He slid them right and left until there was a Humphrey-sized gap at the top of the fence. He climbed up and over the top. But as he cleared the peak, his body weight shifted faster than he'd expected. He rolled over the top and grabbed two fence links. His feet scrambled for a foothold and found none. He hung on by his fingertips. Even through the gloves, the cold metal dug into his skin. His fingers cried that enough was enough, and he let go.

He dropped several feet to the pavement. His feet hit first, but his butt came in a close second, and his back a solid third. He groaned. He was certain this had been easier the last time. Perhaps it was time to get back in the kind of shape he'd been in when he was a fighter ace in the war.

Humphrey made his way down the irregular alleys between the containers. Off to his right, the stacks of a single cargo ship peeked above the row. When he made it to the end of the container jumble, he got a better look at the ship. A tramp steamer that hadn't seen a coat of paint since it had been built floated at the dock. The name on the stern was *Mercury* and Humphrey could not think of a worse name for such a slow ship.

To the left were several small warehouses, the staging area for loads going onboard ships. The Lincoln he'd been following was parked outside the closest warehouse in front of an open loading dock door. Nothing moved in the area around the building.

Humphrey dashed for the warehouse. He climbed the steps to the loading dock and tried the knob on the main door at the building's corner. It was unlocked. He entered the warehouse.

Hanging lights lit the steel building's interior to a level just a bit above dim. Brighter lights illuminated the center of the warehouse floor. Rows of labeled crates seemed to stretch to all four walls. From ahead and to his left came the sounds of creaking wood and hammer blows. Humphrey worked his way through the maze of crates until he neared the source of the noise. Hugging the shadows, he peered around the corner of a stack of crates.

Three men stood by a wooden crate six feet long on both sides and three feet tall. Shredded packing material hung over the sides and a lopsided stack of bagged pecans teetered at the other end of the crate. The larger two of the men wore coats and ties, but the bulges of pistols under their left arms and the scars on their faces told Humphrey they were no businessmen checking on their shipments. Those two were strictly hired muscle, the kind of thugs who would break into an antiques shop and steal a jade hand.

The third man was much shorter and wore a white button-down shirt open at the collar. He had Asian features and a tattoo of a dragon on his right forearm. Humphrey's eyes lit up as he saw that the man held the jade hand.

One of the thugs handed the short man a large towel. The short man wrapped the jade hand in the towel and then placed it in the center of the crate. The three of them filled the rest of the crate with the pecan bags, then nailed the lid back on. When they finished, the short man ordered them all back to the car. The three departed and moments later the Lincoln started and drove off. Whatever these guys were up to, they weren't wasting any time about doing it.

"Well," Humphrey said, "anything y'all can pack, I can unpack. And it ain't stealing if I'm just recovering Rick's property." Humphrey went to the crate.

The shipping label on top was new and listed a recipient in Phnom Penh, Cambodia. That was all the way on the other side of the world. This jade hand was a lot more valuable than he and Rick had guessed if these thieves were international.

The men had left the hammer beside the crate. Just as Humphrey picked it up, the sound of a forklift rumbled outside the open door. Headlights flared into the building.

Humphrey dashed back behind some other crates. The forklift noise grew louder. He crossed his fingers and hoped it was picking up something other than his crate. The engine went to idle and the forks' hydraulics began to whine. That was not the noise he wanted to hear. Humphrey risked a glance around the corner of his crate.

One of the two goons was driving the forklift and had the box with the jade hand lifted several feet off the ground. He reversed and zipped back out the loading dock door.

Humphrey cursed and ran for the dock door. Outside, the forklift made a beeline for the waiting cargo ship.

"Well, Rick can wave that jade hand goodbye," he said.

CHAPTER FOUR

Rick leaned against the counter in the shop as Rose swept the floor around the broken door with short, sharp flicks of the broom. Rick was glad she was taking her fury out on the shop floor instead of giving him the tongue-lashing he certainly deserved.

He knew it was time to extend an olive branch. "I have a broken leg, not a broken arm. I can do that. This is partially my fault."

Rose paused mid-sweep and sighed. "Partially? How about completely? You make deals with people like Matty and Humphrey and suddenly we have hoodlums breaking into our shop."

"Humphrey? He's out there getting the jade hand back for us."

"Supposedly." She sounded more resigned than angry, which was a good sign. "They're all part of this seedy underworld you like to dip your toes into. This time you got me wet as well as your toes. And this time, you've made us dead broke."

"Okay, well, you're right. Looking back on it, buying the hand from Matty might not have been the best idea. It seemed like a sure thing at the time. But Humphrey's going to get it back and we'll turn this whole situation from rainstorm to rainbow."

"Or we'll all get struck by lightning."

Just then, Humphrey knocked on the doorframe with a sheepish look on his face.

"See?" Rick said with triumph. "He's back. Told you."

Humphrey pushed the door open and stepped in. The remaining shards of glass hanging in the door tinkled onto the clean floor. Rose let loose a frustrated growl.

Humphrey was emptyhanded. Rick did not like the look of that. "I trust you have the jade hand in hand?"

"Not exactly," Humphrey said.

"That's a clear *no* in case you missed it, Rick," Rose said.

"I followed 'em to the docks," Humphrey said. 'Snuck up on 'em real good and saw 'em load the hand into a crate. But before I could steal it back, the crate got hauled off and loaded on a ship."

"And there goes our life savings," Rose said. "Off on a trip somewhere in the Atlantic."

"I know where it's going," Humphrey said. "I read the shipping label. It's going to Cambodia."

"Perfect," Rick said. "We'll just go to Cambodia and steal it back."

Rose turned to Rick and rolled her eyes. "Do you even know where Cambodia is?"

Rick had no clue. He pointed vaguely to his upper left. "It's that way."

"It's in Asia," Rose said. "And there's a war going on there."

"That war's up in China," Humphrey said. "Now Rick's idea, it ain't so bad. That tramp steamer ain't fast. I took a detour through the shipping office after leaving the warehouse." He pulled several papers from his pocket. "According to the manifests, it won't dock for over a month. I could get us there before that."

"How could you…" Rose's face fell. She turned to Rick. "Oh, no. You are not flying in that bucket of bolts Humphrey calls an airplane across the Pacific Ocean. I don't think his new hat made him a safer pilot. If Amelia Earhart didn't make it, neither will the two of you."

Humphrey bristled. "Miss Rose, my plane is in top shape. Ain't let either of you down yet."

"I emphasize the 'yet'," Rose said. "And even if you make it, how will you get the crate? So far the idea of stealing back the hand hasn't worked well."

"We'll just ask for it," Rick said.

"And they'll give it to you?"

"Once we hand them our paperwork. Humphrey has all the manifest information so we can fake whatever documents we need. We're Americans, picking up something shipped from America. It couldn't look more legit."

"What about the guys who have the real paperwork?"

"Rosie, you're worrying about details we'll sort out when we get there. The point is we've got ourselves in a financial bind."

"Not *we*. You did that all by yourself."

"Granted. But this is my one chance to reverse it all. Humphrey and I fly in, we grab the jade hand, and we fly home. In and out. It's a sure thing."

Rose took a deep breath and paused. Rick knew that meant she was considering the plan. She turned to Humphrey. "Your plane can make it there and back?"

"Sure as shooting."

"Then we're going," she said.

Rick frowned. "We?"

"If you think I'm letting the two of you fly to the other side of the world by yourselves, you're crazy. That's asking for trouble."

"What kind of trouble could the two of us get into?"

"The list is endless."

"Then we're off," Humphrey said. "They may have a jump on us getting out of port, but the good news is we still have weeks before we need to leave. There may be some deferred maintenance I should get done before we take off."

"And I'll have time to crack this cast and get back into shape," Rick said.

"And I'll start doing some research about Cambodia," Rose said.

CHAPTER FIVE

The next day, the idea of flying around the world to confront thieves sat a bit better with Rose.

She'd agreed to it yesterday, partly because they were in a financial bind, and partly because somehow Rick could make the most outlandish and dangerous scheme seem simple and safe. She couldn't count the number of half-baked plans he'd talked her into over the years. She had to admit, once the danger was in the rearview mirror, she liked the adventure. That was one of the reasons she and Rick were such a good fit, though she'd never admit it to him.

She stepped out of the stairwell and onto the second floor of the Martyn University history building. She had thirty days to learn all the things that her husband and his dopey flyboy pal didn't know about Cambodia, and she was starting today. She went down the hall and knocked on the door of Professor Bartholomew Keene. He called for her to enter.

The small office contained a tidy desk in front of a floor-to-ceiling window. Bookshelves lined both walls. Professor Keene stood before one of them. Rick joked that the professor was a well-rounded man, from his round belly to his round face and even to the round bowler hat he always favored. He smiled and stepped over to greet her.

The professor shook Rose's hand. "Lovely to see you! What brings you to these hallowed halls of academia today?"

"I wanted to get better acquainted with Cambodia and thought you could get me going in the right direction."

"You found some antiques from that area?"

Found, lost, and hope to find again, she thought. "There was one we had our eye on, but I wanted some background to authenticate it."

"Well, you couldn't pick a more fascinating country." The professor went to a shelf and took down a leatherbound volume. "I teach an Overview of Asian History course and it pains me to have to shortchange the Cambodian section. But there are only so many hours in the classroom and the entire continent is fascinating."

He handed her the book. The title read *A History of Southeast Asia*.

"Now this book will tell you quite a bit about Cambodia, but I can give you a quick summary. The place was a substantial kingdom as far back as the 1st century. It peaks in the 12th century as a Hindu state. After a series of catastrophes, King Jayavarman VII converts to Buddhism, and takes his whole country with him, or tries to. Forced religious conversion is fraught with peril, and his empire weakens and shrinks."

"No empire can last forever," Rose said.

"And this one does not. The country is then set upon from all sides for centuries. Even today it is under French rule, though it nominally has its own king. It's one of the rare, peaceful French colonies."

Rose had to keep from sighing in relief over that bit of good news.

The professor took down another book, a world atlas. He flipped through it until he got to Cambodia's pages. He handed the book to Rose. Cambodia was a circular blob wedged between Siam, Laos, and Indochina. The Mekong River ran down the eastern edge past the capital city of Phnom Penh. The other city names were in much smaller print and far apart.

"The capital city is Phnom Penh. The country has a coastline, but the primary access to the city and the interior is through Indochina and up the Mekong."

Rose knew a cargo ship that would soon be making that same passage. "There doesn't seem to be a lot of cities outside the capital."

"No, not now. It's rural and in some places a dense jungle. But in its heyday, the Khmer Empire had cities all over the area and multiple holy sites, massive temples where monks lived and prayed. But after the empire collapsed, the jungle swallowed most of them up forever."

The atlas contained a closeup map of Phnom Penh as well as detailed information about the country.

"May I keep these books for a while?" Rose said.

"Of course." The professor went back to his bookshelf, pulled three other volumes down, then stacked them atop the first. "You should take these as well. The more you know about a culture, the more you will be able to spot the real from the fake in the antiques you find."

The other books were on Hindu and Buddhist religion and a natural history of Asia. Rose lamented having to carry this weighty stack back down the stairs.

She needed to get the professor's take on whether the jade hand could be from that area. "I've heard that Cambodia is a source of precious gems."

"Oh, yes. Wars were sometimes fought over the mines. Pits throughout Southeast Asia have produced rubies, jade, and other stones. You will likely find them if you deal in any jewelry."

Rose was glad to hear that. "I've always thought jade was beautiful."

"So do the locals there. Some even think it has magical powers if carved in the right way and given the proper blessing. If a piece has that kind of superstitious nonsense attached to it, I gather you'll be asked to pay a premium."

It would certainly make a jade hand worth stealing, she thought.

"Thank you," Rose said.

"Not at all. Now if you come across some, well, less expensive pieces that I might use in my classroom, please keep me in mind."

"You are always first on my list, Professor."

The professor beamed. "Splendid."

Rose added the atlas to the stack of books. This was a lot of reading. Lucky for her she had a month to do it, plus one hell of a long airplane ride.

CHAPTER SIX

Over the South China Sea
Four Weeks Later
The old Ford Tri-motor bounced and rocked as
Humphrey banked to skirt the edge of a rising
thundercloud. The wings flexed and moaned. Rick sat in
the co-pilot seat and tried to mask how nervous he felt.

A lifetime of bluffing at card games and making
shady business deals had inspired Rick's personal motto
of "fake it until you figure it out." It had come in handy
over-and-over again, especially when he had proposed
this trip a month ago. He'd professed to be confident and
enthusiastic about the Tri-motor's reliability, but that had
been a front. He had significant doubts that the old bird
could fly them halfway around the world. Even now,
after their final stop in Singapore, he fingered his life
vest every time he looked out the window at the choppy
South China Sea.

Rose stepped up from the rear of the plane. Rick gave
her credit for being a good sport during their island-
hopping trip across the Pacific. He was glad he'd
married someone who didn't fall apart in the face of a
little hardship, and they'd had more than a little during
this bumpy flight between barely-developed island
towns.

"How far out are we?" she said.

Rick blanched. Technically, as the co-pilot he was
supposed to be keeping track of their position. But
Humphrey's instructions about how to determine their
location by the stars hadn't sunk in and he hadn't
admitted it. He'd barely been able to follow the wind
adjustments to the desired compass heading. Right now,

he was only sure they should be headed west, and they were.

"Not too long now," Humphrey said. "Ought to see some coastline anytime now."

"That will be a relief," she said. "All this open water makes me nervous."

"See, Rosie," Rick said. "I told you that you could trust this plane."

Rose fingered his life vest. "Yes, look at all this trust wrapped around your neck."

"I just find the yellow brings out my eyes," Rick said.

"Humphrey, I didn't see your passport with the paperwork back here," Rose said.

"Won't be needing one," Humphrey said. "We're landing in a private airfield just outside of the city."

"I think the French authorities won't make exceptions for that."

"The French authorities ain't gonna know," Humphrey said.

"If we're going to sneak out with the jade hand," Rick said, "we should sneak in to get it."

Rose exhaled a frustrated sigh. Rose's reaction was why Rick usually kept the sketchier details of his plans from her.

"And you're sure we can trust this Charya Thang person?" Rose said to Humphrey.

Charya was Humphrey's contact in Cambodia who was going to meet them at the plane. This was a necessity since as far as Rick was concerned, the local language was indecipherable.

"Of course I am," Humphrey said.

"How did you meet him?"

"He was recommended by a friend of a friend."

"Hard to beat bona fides like that," Rose said.

"We *are* on the other side of the world, Rosie," Rick said. "You have to trust someone."

"Even when in an untrustworthy endeavor?" Rose said.

"Especially then," Rick said.

"Land ho!" Humphrey called out.

Out the front windshield, the Indochinese coast appeared. Small fishing boats dotted the water. A mile behind them, waves lapped against a narrow beach. The plane flew over the boats and beach. Inland, what looked like endless plots of green rice patties stretched out across a seemingly perfectly flat land. As the plane roared over, workers in the fields wearing conical thatched hats looked up in curiosity.

Rick pulled out the map of the area Humphrey had given him. It creaked as he unfolded it and age had yellowed the paper and made it brittle. "This map seems a little old."

"This ain't a part of the world that changes all that often." Humphrey squinted out the windshield. "And there's our river!"

He laid the plane into a righthand bank and then aimed it for a wide, muddy river up ahead. Once they came to it, Humphrey followed it northwest.

"This here's the Mekong," he said. "Gonna take us straight to Phnom Penh."

In a short time, the city appeared on the left bank of the river. The first aspect of it that struck Rick as different was how low the buildings were. Few, if any, were taller than two stories, most only one, though high, peaked roofs were common. Most of the streets were laid out in a neat grid and several docks along the river had steamers tied up at them. Those docks were the part of the city that Rick cared about.

The engine outside Rick's window stumbled and belched out a cloud of black smoke. The needle on the oil pressure gauge for that engine began to drop. Rick gripped the dash.

"You hear that?" he said hooking a thumb over his shoulder.

The muscles in Humphrey's neck were tight as harp strings. "You bet."

Rick pointed to the dropping oil pressure. "And you see that?"

"Looking like we've blown a seal." Humphrey throttled back the engine and feathered the propeller. The plane lurched and Humphrey wrestled with the controls to level it back out.

"Can we fly on two engines?" Rose said.

"Of course we can," Rick said. He turned to Humphrey. "We can, right?"

"Absolutely."

Rick could always tell when a man was bluffing, and the worried look on Humphrey's face didn't back up his reassuring answer. Humphrey angled the plane west and skirted the south side of the city. About fifteen harrowing miles later, Humphrey called out that he had the airfield in sight.

Rick didn't see anything resembling an airfield. What he did see was a tall bamboo pole in the middle of a field with a strip of red cloth tied at the top. "You mean that place there?"

"What did you expect? I've landed in tougher spots." Humphrey sent the plane into a jerking right hand turn to the pasture. He fought the controls and leveled the plane. "'Course I done it with three engines."

Rick looked over his shoulder. "Rose, you'd better—"

She wasn't there.

"Put on my seatbelt?" she said from back in the plane. "Already done."

Rick was no certified pilot, but he'd completed enough landings with Humphrey in the Tri-motor to know that this one wasn't going by the book. Their speed was too high, the engines were still going full throttle, and the descent rate was too fast. This landing was not going to end well. He tightened his own seatbelt.

"Did I ever tell you about the time I landed in no-man's-land during the war? It was as rough as this pasture."

"Yes, and you said you balled up the SPAD you were flying doing it."

"Sure enough did. But that's why I'll know how to do it right this time."

Humphrey brought the plane in fast and steep. Rick saw a lot more control adjustments and noticed a lot more pitching and rolling than usual. The ground seemed to come up fast.

"Aw, damn it," Humphrey muttered.

Rick didn't want to know what that meant. He closed his eyes.

Both engines stopped. The nose of the plane pitched up. The tailwheel struck the ground and bounced, then the main landing gear hit. The plane bounded down the field like a stone being skipped over a pond. Every impact sent shivers through the aircrafts' frame. Somewhere in the main cabin, rivets popped.

Rick opened his eyes. Another bounce made him bite his tongue and he yelped. The plane settled fully onto the ground, rolling forward.

And right at a drainage ditch.

Humphrey and Rick both stomped on the brakes. The wheels locked up but kept skidding forward as they plowed ruts through the soft ground. The tires dropped into the drainage ditch. The plane rotated up on its nose and Rick slid forward against his seatbelt. All he saw through the windshield was grass and mud. The tail rose to almost perpendicular.

Almost.

The tail hung in the air for a second, then dropped back down to the ground. It smashed into the earth so hard that the impact made everything in the cargo area jump off the cabin floor and crash back down. Rick hoped Rose hadn't done the same. He unbuckled his seatbelt and climbed back into the cabin.

Rose was still strapped into her chair. Her face was ghost-white, her eyes closed.

Rick dashed to her, knelt, and placed a hand on her cheek. She did not respond.

"Rosie, Rosie girl. Are you okay?"

Rose's eyes fluttered open. "Yes, I think so. Something hit me in the head."

Rick touched the back of her head. Her hair was wet and sticky. He pulled his hand away. Blood smeared his fingertips. Rick's heart sank.

"You got a bump there." He pulled a handkerchief from his pocket and placed it on the back of her head. "Here, hold this while I find some water."

Humphrey entered the cabin. He cringed at the sight of Rose. "You all right, Miss Rose?"

"Yes." Her voice sounded stronger. "Just a bump on the head."

"I hope the plane came through all that as well as you did." Humphrey popped the door and jumped outside. Hot, humid air filled the cabin like an invading army.

Rick rummaged around the jumble of supplies in the cabin looking for water. Rose stood up, hand still pressing his handkerchief.

"I'm okay," she said. "Just get me out of this plane and back on solid ground."

Rick jumped out the door and landed hard on spongy earth. Rose stood in the doorway. He reached up and grabbed her waist. He lifted her up, swiveled around, and set her down gently.

Humphrey stepped up behind them. "Well, we lucked out. The props stopped horizontal enough that they didn't hit the ground. Tailwheel took the impact like a champ, don't think it's bent none. Once I fire up an engine I can pull it out of that ditch. But unless I get the Number One engine running, that's as far as we're going to go."

"You said we could fly on two engines," Rose said.

"Sure enough. But we can't *take off* on two engines, especially with a full load of fuel. Gonna need to see where all that oil leaked from and patch it up."

"Maybe Charya knows someone who can help," Rick said. "He ought to be along momentarily."

Rose pointed past the rudder and across the field. "Was he supposed to bring people with guns?"

Rick went to the tail and looked over the alerion. A trio of men were walking toward the aircraft. The two on the outside were armed with rifles.

CHAPTER SEVEN

Every misgiving Rose had ignored about this stupid plan came screaming back to her. The trip had been miserable. Humphrey's rickety plane had crash landed and left them stranded in Cambodia. And now their welcoming party consisted of men with guns. She vowed to never let Rick talk her into another scheme.

The two shirtless men on the outside wore something that looked like a skirt, but there was nothing feminine about them at all. They were all muscle from their necks down to their sandaled feet. Their faces were masks of grim determination. The rifles in their hands were vintage bolt-action models, but looked well-maintained and lethal.

The smaller Cambodian man in the center wore Western-style clothing with a loose white button-down shirt and dark slacks. While the other men's hair was unkempt, the man in the middle's was slicked back with a sharp part on the right.

He motioned to the other two and they spread out, looking like they were cutting off any possible escape for Rose and the others. The unarmed man headed straight for the Tri-motor's tail and he wasn't smiling.

"He doesn't look happy," Rick said.

"How happy would you be if someone crashed a plane on your property?" Rose said.

"If you can walk away," Humphrey said, "it's a landing, not a crash."

Rick and Rose retreated to the cabin door. Humphrey set out to intercept the leader. The two stopped a few feet apart. The man sized up Humphrey.

"It seems there is a good chance of rain today," the man said.

Of all the things Rose thought the man might say, a weather report was not on the list.

"I haven't seen rain in over a week," Humphrey said.

Rose was even more mystified at Humphrey's ridiculous response.

The man smiled. One tooth was crowned in gold. "You are Humphrey?"

"And you're Charya? Pleasure to meet ya."

The two men shook hands. Rose exhaled in relief. Those must have been some kind of coded recognition phrases.

Rick stepped up and shook Charya's hand. "Rick Sinclair. And that's my wife, Rose."

Rose stepped over and shook Charya's hand as well. "My pleasure."

Charya waved at his two men. They both visibly relaxed and Rose finally did the same.

Charya gave the cockeyed Tri-motor a sideways glance. "I was told you were an experienced pilot."

"I was told this was an improved landing strip," Humphrey said. "The fact that the plane is upright and undamaged ought to prove I'm an experienced pilot."

"You'll need to get it out of that ditch and into the tree line if you want to avoid a lot of unwanted attention. This land is part of an abandoned rubber plantation. Not many people venture out here, but if they do, they'll sure notice an airplane parked in a field."

"Pull her out of that there ditch, and I can taxi her over to the trees, but I'll need to work on her a bit to get her able to takeoff. Something amiss in one engine."

Rose rolled her eyes at that understatement.

"Before we begin," Charya said. "There is the matter of my payment."

"Tucked into the tail of my plane behind a hidden panel," Humphrey said. "Four cases of true American whiskey distilled by one Mr. James Beam."

Charya pointed to one of his men. "Go check that it survived the landing."

The man nodded and entered the plane.

"We were smuggling booze across the world?" Rose whispered to Rick. "And how did you two get your hands on that much liquor?"

"That's nothing you need to worry about. We know a guy in the business."

"The business of stealing whiskey?" Rose said.

The henchman stuck his head back out of the plane and gave Charya a thumbs up and a short sentence in Cambodian.

Charya smiled. "Very good. Now you are going to intercept a shipment at the docks. Let me see the paperwork you will be using."

Humphrey pulled a piece of paper from his pocket and handed it to Charya. Charya looked it over and his eyes narrowed. "All this information is correct?"

"Copied straight from the shipping records in Savannah," Rick said.

"This addressee, Rathanak Khong, he is not a man to be trifled with. He has an extensive business empire, and he neither came by it, nor holds onto it, honestly. His rivals tend to go missing and are never found."

"Couldn't ask for a guy more deserving to be robbed," Rick said.

"Or more dangerous once he has been," Rose said.

"She is correct," Charya said. "As soon as you have what you seek, you should fly away immediately."

"That's why I want to get a good look at that engine right off," Humphrey said.

The two henchmen exited the aircraft carrying crates of liquor. They disappeared over the top of a hill.

"One bit of business done," Charya said. "Those two gave me the willies."

"Those weren't your men?" Rose said.

"Hardly. They work for the liquor buyer and are here to guard those crates. I'm a solo operation. Much safer in this line of work."

That confirmed for Rose how shady Charya's line of work really was.

"I'll bring my truck around," Charya said. "We'll pull the plane free, then we'll all go into the city."

"I'd best stay here and start working on the plane," Humphrey said. "No one's going to bother me none, right?"

"The plantation buildings burned down decades ago, killing a bunch of workers and the whole family. The locals think the place is haunted by vengeful spirits, so they steer clear of the entire property. You should be okay for a while."

Rose didn't like the idea of her and Rick being isolated and under the control of someone who was way too comfortable surrounded by armed goons. She gave Rick a wide-eyed look. He nodded.

"We should stay and help him out," Rick said. "The ship isn't due for two days."

"The *Mercury* had favorable winds," Charya said. "It has already docked."

CHAPTER EIGHT

It took a few tries, but Charya's truck finally pulled the Tri-motor free of the ditch. They all stayed nearby while Humprey taxied it closer to the trees. Then the four of them worked to cover the wings and body with dark green tarps from inside the plane. True to Charya's description, the two guards just sat in the open back of the truck beside the liquor crates the entire time.

Rose turned to Rick. "What a coincidence that Humphrey carries camouflage covers for his plane in the cargo area."

"Camouflage?" Rick said with feigned shock. "No, those are, uh, tent pieces he uses for shade when he has to do maintenance. Army surplus from the war, that kind of thing."

"Uh huh."

Then Rick and Rose boarded the truck for the ride to the city. Rose sat by the passenger door of the old truck with her husband beside her while Charya drove. The two men and the liquor stayed in the open back.

At first, Rose thought the trip captivating. The fields and lush jungles in the countryside seemed to come in endless shades of lovely green. The motion of the truck sent a breeze across her face and made the stifling heat and humidity bearable. Blue sky peeked out between bright white clouds.

Then they came to the outskirts of Phnom Penh. The truck slowed, the wind stopped, and the full weight of the tropical weather crashed down on her. The buildings they passed ranged from traditional thatch and bamboo to similar designs using more modern construction materials, though all of the materials looked more scavenged than purchased. Scantily clad men and women sat on stoops and walked the streets. Rose guessed there wasn't running water or electricity in a single home.

"Hard times bring people from the countryside into the city," Charya said. "They have to make their own place to live. I'm sure America is just the same."

Even the roughest places in American cities were far better than this, but Rose wasn't about to tell Charya that.

The road improved to something resembling concrete and they passed into Phnom Penh proper. Wide streets cut straight lines through the city. Sidewalks fronted two-story masonry buildings that would have looked at home in any town in France. Behind them rose the pointed, square spires of the temples she'd seen from the air. The streets teemed with people and ox-driven carts and bicycles outnumbered automobiles.

"Now for all this 'civilization'," Charya said, "we thank the French. They assumed we wanted to mimic the streets of Paris."

"It seems quite nice," Rose said.

"It would be, in France. These are not buildings designed for our climate like our traditional homes. These are hot and claustrophobic."

The truck pulled into an alleyway and then stopped at a loading dock behind one building. The men jumped out and began to unload the liquor. Charya, Rose, and Rick left the cab. Charya went over, and unlocked the door. The three of them entered and the men disappeared down the street carrying the liquor crates.

Charya led them through a small stock room and into a shop. Dust motes floated in the light from the front windows and lazy fans churned the air near the ceiling. The room smelled of incense and polished wood. A variety of Cambodian artifacts from stone carvings to wooden figurines to traditional headdresses and garments filled rows of tables.

"This is your shop?" Rick said.

"Yes, I resell antiquities collected from around the country."

"What a coincidence. So do we."

Charya looked wary. "What is it you are stealing from the warehouse?"

"Stealing sounds so criminal," Rick said. "A piece from *our* shop was stolen. The thieves shipped it here to the man on the paperwork. We're just trying to get it back."

Charya shrugged. "It's none of my business anyway. I'm just the paid guide for this trip."

"Seriously," Rose said. "My husband is telling the truth."

She wanted to add "for once" but restrained herself.

"The ship's early arrival may work to your advantage," Charya said. "Khong lives inland somewhere up the Mekong. It is common for news of early arriving cargo ships to travel slowly, if at all. He has likely planned to arrive here when the ship docks. With any luck at all, he will come two days late, and find his shipment missing."

"And halfway back to America by then," Rick said.

"Then we need to be there as soon as possible, just in case Khong has gotten word of the updated schedule. Let me see the paperwork you have on the crate."

Rick handed him the papers Humphrey had given him.

Charya scoffed. "A shipment of pecans? What are those?"

"A kind of tree nut," Rose said.

"Never heard of it."

"They're all the rage where we come from," Rose said. "Pecan pie is a favorite."

"You make pies out of nuts?" Charya sighed. "And I thought French food was ridiculous."

"According to Humphrey," Rick said, "the artifact is packed between those sacks of pecans."

"Good choice. With pecans on the invoice, Khong knew that no one would steal the crate. Now you are going to need some customs stamps on those invoices for the warehouse manager to let you take that crate."

Charya took the invoice over to his desk, opened a top drawer, and sorted through some rubber stamps. He selected one, inked it on a pad, and stamped a Cambodian customs clearance on the invoice.

"You're a Cambodian customs officer?" Rick said.

"As far as you know, yes."

Rose poked Rick in the ribs. "That's what you always say when you're lying."

"See, I liked the cut of this guy's jib from the moment we met."

Charya walked back over and handed Rick the papers. He checked his watch. "We have time for dinner. We will step down the street and I will introduce you to Cambodian cuisine. By the time we are finished, the *Mercury's* cargo should be unloaded and waiting for Rick and I to retrieve the crate in the warehouse. Then I will take you straight back to pick up your wife, then back to your airplane."

"Oh, no," Rose said. "I'm going with you to the warehouse to get the crate."

"If you want extra attention," Charya said, "having an American woman coming to the warehouse would be the perfect way to do it. The docks are a rough place where men do all the business."

"Nonsense," Rose said. "I'm in warehouses in America all the time."

"But you are not in America. Fifteen minutes after you enter the gate, every worker in the complex will know there's a Western woman entering that warehouse. Men loyal to Khong, or even ones wishing to curry favor, will be investigating."

"Rosie," Rick said, "I hate to have to agree with him, but he's right on this one. It's safer for all of us if you wait here."

Little infuriated Rose more than being patronized, or worse, marginalized because she was a woman. But she had to admit this was not the time to light the torch for women's rights in Cambodia. "Fine. I'll wait here."

"We'll be in and out and back in no time," Rick said with a smile. "Trust me."

Rose looked into his eyes but couldn't tell whether this was one of his "fake-it-until-you-figure-it-out" moments or not. This whole adventure was getting sketchier by the minute and for once she was looking forward to a long trip in Humphrey's Tri-motor.

***

Back at the plane, Humphrey shined a flashlight up into the open cowling on the #3 engine. The canvas draped over the wing might have blocked the sun, but it also blocked the breeze, and the humid air felt thick as molasses. The enclosure also seemed to have convened a congress of ravenous mosquitos who were keen on treating Humphrey like a buffet. He slapped at his neck for the dozenth time and his hand came away bloody.

"Serves you right," he muttered.

He wiped the leaked oil off the engine. A seep reappeared at the #2 cylinder head gasket. He soon saw why. The gasket had cracked and left a gap around the bolt.

At home, this would be a quick fix. Humphrey had a few salvaged engines in a shed and an assortment of new gaskets. A few scavenged parts and a gasket later, he'd be up and flying.

But he wasn't home. He was on the edge of an abandoned rubber plantation in Cambodia with no idea how far away the closest aircraft parts store might be. He was certain it wasn't just down the road a piece.

CHAPTER NINE

Charya stopped his truck a block from the gates to the dock warehouses. The sun had set a while ago and the lighting around the dock area was marginal, but Rick could see that there were several warehouses lining the shore by the docks. He could make out the illuminated mast and bridge of the *Mercury* at the dock.

"Your wife was angry about staying back at the shop," Charya said.

"You think that was angry?" Rick said. "That was just perturbed. Call her a 'dame' and then you'll see angry. I know her, and I'm certain she knew you were right. It bugs her to get treated as someone inferior when she's one of the smartest people I've ever met."

Charya pulled out the forged manifest documents. "Khong used Nibs and Worthington Limited for the shipping. That's a British firm so the good news is we'll be dealing with an English-speaking Brit."

That was a relief for Rick. He always felt uneasy doing any kind of deal through an interpreter since he was always a little paranoid about the conversation not going as the interpreter said it was.

"What's the bad news?"

"It won't be someone I've dealt with before. Nibs and Worthington generally handle shipping well out of my price range."

They drove into the dock area and stopped in the shadows behind a warehouse boasting a big NIBS AND WORTHINGTON, LTD. sign. They left the truck and Rick followed Charya to the door.

"Let me get the conversation started," Charya said.

"Be my guest."

The warehouse door opened to a shabby office that contained two messy desks, rows of filing cabinets, and a faded world map on one wall. The other three walls of the office were large windows onto the warehouse. Rows of crates half-filled the area. The ceiling height and the stairway outside the office indicated there was a second floor as well.

A small, middle-aged man looked up at them from one of the desks. He wore round, rimless glasses and had a moustache so bushy that it would make a walrus proud. His rumpled shirt and red-rimmed eyes said he was here much later than he usually was. The nameplate on the desk said he was Mr. Nibs.

With a bit of a flourish, Charya handed the man the fake manifest. "I'm Mr. Charya Thang, this is Mr. Sinclair. We're here for this crate."

Nibs looked confused. "That was quick. I only left a message at Mr. Khong's estate an hour ago."

Damn, Rick thought. *The cat's out of the bag on this already.*

"In case of an early arrival, Mr. Sinclair was waiting in the city," Charya said. "The sooner the crate is on the way to Mr. Khong's estate, the happier Mr. Khong will be."

"I'm much happier when he's happy." He gave the two of them, especially Rick a visual inspection. "Say, you aren't the usual chaps who do this sort of thing."

"Quite right," Rick said. "I'm the one who shipped the crate out of Savannah. I made sure it got on the boat in one piece and I'm here to make sure it got off the boat in one piece."

Nibs looked wary. Rick flashed him his passport and pointed to the Savannah address.

"If you were so worried about it," Nibs said, "why didn't you sail with it?"

"On a slow cargo steamer? Would you?"

"I quite see your point there." He turned back to Charya. "And what's your role in this?"

"I'm just the hired driver. Pick up, drop off, carry bags and boxes."

Rick had sat at enough poker tables to tell by the look on a man's face if one of Rick's bluffs wasn't working. Nibs' face said this tall tale was falling short.

Nibs eyed the paperwork. "Pecans? Aren't those some kind of nut?"

"And they're delicious. I'm afraid the steamer crew might have gotten into them."

"If it's pecans, more likely rats did."

Why does everyone in this country denigrate pecans? Rick thought.

Nibs looked over the paperwork again. "This seems in order. But how did you get customs clearance at this hour?"

This charade was unraveling faster than a cheap sweater.

"My brother works in the customs office," Charya said. "He …uh…expedites things for a fee. I should introduce you."

"Mr. Nibs, we're not picking up the crate," Rick said. "I'm just inspecting it, and want to do it before the *Mercury* weighs anchor. We both know of Mr. Khong's low tolerance for failure. If something happened to this crate in transit, I want the captain held accountable, not me, and not you."

Nibs' brow furrowed at the mention of running afoul of Khong. Rick had just assumed any criminal bigwig was a bully. Lucky for him Khong was true to type.

"Very well," Nibs said. "Go ahead and inspect the crate. It's in Mr. Khong's secure area, along with yesterday's shipment the courier delivered. A forklift driver just set the crate inside the fencing before clocking out. I was just about to relock it."

"Thank you," Charya said.

He and Rick left the office for the warehouse. They headed down one aisle.

"So where's Khong's secure area?" Rick said.

"How would I know?" Charya said. "But I wasn't about to ask."

"Okay," Rick said. "Take a left at that red crate and stop."

They made the turn and stopped. Rick counted to three and peered back around the crate and down the aisle. Nibs was on the phone in his office.

Rick turned back to Charya. "He didn't buy our story. He picked up a phone as soon as we were out of sight. He's either calling to check on his poor sick mother, or he's dialed Khong to ask if he knows who we are."

"Then we need to find that crate fast."

"Humphrey told me what it looks like." Rick reached down to an empty pallet nearby and pulled off one of the broken slats. "You stay here and watch the office. If Khong or any of his goons step into the warehouse, beat one of these crates with this slat. Then take off and I'll meet you outside at the truck."

Charya took the slat and nodded. As he turned to keep an eye on the office, Rick took off down the aisle. At the end of the row, he took a right turn to follow the wall. He figured if Khong had his own secure area, he'd have it up against at least one solid wall.

It only took him a few minutes to confirm he was correct. He spied the crate of pecans on his left inside a fenced-in area about fifteen feet square. Shelving along the wall held some smaller packages. As Nibs had promised, the door in the fence was still unlocked.

Rick dashed in and went straight to the crate. The good news was it was still sealed. The bad news was it was still sealed and he had nothing to pry it open with. A broken pallet leaned up against the fencing, but that wasn't going to be of any use. He began a frantic search of the shelves in the hope of finding a screwdriver or a crowbar. At this point he'd settle for a sledgehammer.

A padlocked wooden shipping box two feet long on each side was the largest item on the shelf. This had to be the courier-delivered item that Nibs had mentioned. A seal stamped into the side of the box had been painted over, but Rick still recognized it. It was the sword and shield emblem of the Grand Duchy Museum, the same emblem on the bag Matty's jade hand came in.

That was too big a coincidence to be a coincidence.

Rick gave the small lock a quick inspection. It was nothing impressive, just something to keep the courier from opening the box, so whatever was inside was valuable. Now he *really* wished he had a crowbar.

He did have that broken pallet.

He took the box over to the wall and set it on the floor. Rick grabbed one of the stouter pallet boards and set it against the latch and lock on the box. Then he hopped up and came down on it like he was driving a spade into hard soil.

The lock broke away with a crunch. Rick tossed aside the board, picked the box up off the floor, and set it on the pecan crate.

He opened the top. It was stuffed with excelsior. He plucked the packing material out.

Inside the box was the jade hand.

He grinned with relief at his good luck, then realized what he saw made no sense. The hand had to be in the still-sealed pecan crate. Besides, this was delivered yesterday.

Rick took out the hand and examined it. The workmanship was just as exquisite as the hand he'd seen in his shop. The difference was that one was a right hand and this one was a left hand. He'd lay odds that the same person carved them, from the same deposit of jade.

There might be an entire statue around here somewhere, he thought. *Wouldn't that be a prize to take home?*

CHAPTER TEN

Back in the office, Clifford Nibs patted sweat from his forehead with a handkerchief. But for once tropical heat wasn't the cause of his perspiration. It was nervous worry. He hadn't bought the story those two men had just tried to sell him. But alone in the warehouse, he was in no position to do anything about it.

Khong wasn't the kind of man you could disappoint and live to tell about it. If only half the stories of his intolerance for failure were true, Clifford was already a dead man. His only hope was that Khong's shipment of pecans, or whatever was really in that crate, didn't make it out of the warehouse. That meant Khong's men had better get here before the two thieves in the warehouse escaped.

The sound of vehicles came from outside. Nibs went to the window. Two sedans were parked in front of the door. Four men got out. It was too dark to see their faces, but the size of them either said gangsters or gorillas escaped from a zoo. Khong's men had arrived. Nibs went back to his desk, unsure if he should feel relieved or even more terrified.

Then the door burst open. Four rough-looking men came in with all the grace of a cattle stampede. Nibs recognized the leader, Oliver Metcalfe, one of the group of thugs Khong had recruited out of British Army deserters. The Brits grew them bigger and beefier than they did in Cambodia, and Khong liked having every advantage he could.

"Mr. Khong said to get here fast," Metcalfe said. "What's going on?"

"Two men came in here looking for the shipment that just unloaded. A local and an American. Their paperwork looked suspicious, so I called Mr. Khong to confirm it."

"And you let them in anyway?" Metcalfe said.

"Two of them and one of me. What could I do?"

Metcalfe shook his head in disgust. "Who was the local?"

"Said his name was Charya Thang."

"We know him." Metcalfe turned to one of the thugs. "Blackie, get to Charya's shop and wait there in case he somehow gets past us. Look around inside and see if he has anything else Mr. Khong might find interesting."

Nibs was thrilled that all these problems were being taken off his hands.

"Where are those two thieves now?" Metcalfe said.

"Out looking for the shipment of pecans in Mr. Khong's secure area."

"But it's locked, right?"

Nibs winced. "I'm afraid it is still open. The delivery had just been made and I was on my way to lock it when—"

Metcalfe cut off his sentence with a piledriver-like punch to Nibs' gut. Nibs moaned and bent over.

"That's for leaving Mr. Khong's belongings unlocked and unsupervised. You'd better start praying we find those two before they take something that doesn't belong to them."

***

From out in the warehouse came the sharp crack of wood against wood.

Rick's heart skipped a beat at hearing the warning signal. He and Charya were about to have visitors.

One thing every good gambler knows is to quit a table when the luck starts to run cold. Rick's luck in this warehouse had done just that. It was time to leave.

He gave the pecan crate a rueful look. The hand was still in there.

But he did have the equivalent in his hands right now. If stealing back an item stolen from him was justified, stealing back the equivalent had to be as well. As long as he flew back to Savannah with a jade hand, he could say mission accomplished.

Now all he had to do was let whoever had entered the warehouse pass him by so he could double-back to the door and get out of here. That would be easy in the maze of crates in the warehouse. He stepped out of the fenced area.

"Don't move!" someone yelled.

The shout came from down the aisle to his right. He turned to see two beefy-looking men a hundred yards away. These two were not Cambodians. They'd have looked right at home driving gangsters around Chicago. One of them pulled a pistol from his waistband.

Rick bolted in the opposite direction.

The pistol fired and the blast echoed in the building. A bullet struck a crate to Rick's left and sent splinters into the aisle in front of him.

"Twit!" one of the men said. The accent was British. "There's gasoline drums about. You trying to kill us?"

The sound of pounding feet came from behind and Rick pushed himself harder. Problem Number One was that the exit from the building was in the opposite direction. Problem Number Two was that the footsteps were getting closer. Those two goons could sprint.

At the end of the aisle, a ladder ran up the wall and through an opening to the second floor. Rick saw no escape down here, maybe he could lose these two on the second floor. This was the kind of longshot Rick always bet on.

He made it to the bottom of the ladder, stuffed the jade hand in his shirt, and began a frantic scramble up the rungs.

At two-thirds of the way up, he felt the ladder shake and heard the clang of heavy shoes on the bottom rung. Rick's legs and arms ached but he kept climbing.

"One more move and I'll blow your head off!"

The voice sounded way too close. Rick was near to the opening to the next floor. He stopped and looked down over his shoulder. One of the goons had paused halfway up the ladder. He hung on with one hand, but in the other had a pistol aimed at Rick.

'Nothing but wall behind you," the thug said. "Nothing to keep me from shooting you now."

It looked like Rick's longshot hadn't come in.

"You've got me," Rick said. "This is what you want, though."

Rick pulled the hand out of his shirt and held it out.

"Blimey," the thug still on the ground said. "He's got one of the hands."

"Shoot me and I'll drop it," Rick said. "And it's worthless in a hundred pieces."

This standoff took the goons by surprise. It seemed they knew not only about the jade hands, but how important they were to whoever they were working for.

"You're going to climb down," the thug on the ladder said. "Nice and easy like, and hand over that jade."

"I'm in a generous mood." Rick held the hand out over the thug. "You can just have it."

He let the hand go. It fell right at the thug on the ladder. He dropped his gun and grabbed for the jade sculpture. He caught it, but not before he twisted himself too far out of balance. One foot slipped off a rung, then his left hand did the same. He fell backward and dropped ten feet to the ground. He hit the concrete with a thud and did not move.

"Charlie!" The other thug ran to his henchman buddy.

Rick rocketed up the last few rungs and into the second floor. He turned to find a hiding place.

This floor of the warehouse was empty. But he knew as soon as the second goon made it up here, it would become a shooting gallery. There was the set of stairs at the far end that went down to the office. Rick could be one long sprint away from getting out of this alive.

The goon's voice came up through the ladder opening. "Monty, Charlie's dead. The American's on the second floor. Go up the stairs there and cut him off. I'll go up the ladder."

There was a third man down there, maybe more. That thug would probably be up the far stairwell before Rick even got there.

A set of wide double doors stood in the middle of the side wall. Rick dashed for them. He made it to one and pulled it open.

He faced the river, which the warehouse lighting left mostly in shadows. These were loading doors and a rusty boom arm stretched out through them and then out over the water. A hanging pulley was able to run down that rail and be used to winch cargo straight from the deck of a ship and into the warehouse. But while there was dark water thirty feet away at the end of the boom, straight down there awaited a lot of very hard-looking concrete.

"There he is!" one of the thugs shouted.

A pistol fired and a bullet chipped the wooden floor at Rick's feet. It was time to ante up or fold.

He stepped back and pulled the release that linked the pulley to the positioning chain. With the pulley free to slide along the boom, he ran forward as fast as he could. More gunshots rang out, this time from both ends of the warehouse. As Rick reached the threshold, he pushed harder and sailed out into space.

The wheels that guided the pulleys along the boom screeched. Shedding rust tinkled down on Rick's head and back. Rick realized that with no cargo on the second level, this whole setup might not have been used for a long time.

His fears were confirmed as the pulley slowed. His arms were burning and he was pretty sure he'd raised blisters on his palms. He swung his legs like a kid on a swing, and tried to generate more momentum. All he managed to do was add a slow twist to the pulley's motion. Halfway down the boom, the pulleys ground to a halt with Rick facing the second-floor door.

In it stood the goon who'd been chasing him. He had his pistol leveled at Rick.

Rick couldn't tell if he'd gone out far enough to land in deep enough water to cushion his fall, or if he'd land in water at all. But while the drop might or might not kill him, the next bullet out of that thug's gun certainly would.

Rick let go.

The thug fired. The pulley exploded and went sailing off into the darkness.

The drop seemed to take forever. Galloping dread over the impact threatened to make Rick sick. He locked his ankles together and held his nose. Another gunshot sounded from the door above him just as he hit the water.

The impact sent a shockwave from his ankles up through his spine to his skull. The Mekong was bathwater warm and silty. Rick clamped his eyelids shut, afraid that whatever was swirling around out there could blind him. He immediately began to kick and swim upward.

His lungs begged to exhale as he fought his way to the surface. Or what he hoped would be the surface.

With his eyes closed and the disorienting impact, he really couldn't be sure.

A few bubbles escaped his lips. He clamped his jaw tighter, and fought the need to exhale with sheer willpower. He'd soon lose that fight for sure.

Then his head broke the surface. He exhaled so deeply that he almost went back under. Rick flailed his arms in the water to keep himself afloat as he inhaled over and over. The river reeked of dead fish and fuel oil. He felt a greasy sheen on his face. He wiped his eyes and opened them.

The current was faster than it had seemed. He was already downstream of the warehouse and out of pistol range. But he was also heading straight for the still-docked *Mercury*.

The vessel's bow loomed high overhead. He tried to swim out of the way, but between hanging from the pulley's hook and working hard to not drown, his flaccid arms were spent. Rick struck the ship's hull. The current forced him down the ship's waterline along the outboard side. Pockets of rust and sharp barnacles tore at his clothes and pricked his skin. He tried to push away, but the current drove him back each time, like the ship was a magnet and he was an iron filing.

From the stern of the ship came a thrum of deep splashes. Dockside light lit the ship's raised stern and revealed the slowly-turning twin screw propellers. Each had to be ten feet across.

Rick was headed right for one of them. Even if it didn't cut him in half, the prop would drag him under and this time he'd never surface. Rick felt like a slab of beef heading for a slicer.

CHAPTER ELEVEN

Rose paced around Charya's antiques shop, getting angrier as the wall clock notched the minutes since her husband and Charya had left her here. She did not like feeling helpless or useless and right now she felt both. While she understood why the two of them went without her, she sure didn't like it.

She also didn't like being alone in the shop after dark. She'd double checked that the doors were locked, but it was still unnerving to be alone in a strange shop in a strange city in a strange country.

The more she wandered around the shop, the less impressed with it she became. She certainly would not call it an antiques shop, no matter what Charya said. The first two aisles by the window contained older items, but none seemed more than ten years old, many were damaged, and all of them carried a heavy coating of dust. Nothing here seemed to have even been browsed over in a long time.

The other two-thirds of the shop looked more like the set of a horror film than an antique store. There were statues of what she could only guess were deities: a woman with multiple arms, a man with what looked like an elephant trunk, a trident-carrying deity with something she could not make out wrapped around its neck. Blocks of carved stone contained fragments from larger scenes. There were also other artifacts whose purpose or provenance she could only guess at.

The table along the back wall contained a variety of brass incense burners. Beside them were small flip-top wooden boxes. She opened a few to find that each was filled with a different incense for those burners. One incense in a red box was so pungent it made her wince.

This section of the shop gave her chills, as if these pieces had a darkness about them. She was certain that many of them had been stolen from archeological sites, but that wasn't what was triggering her. There was something *wrong* with the things in this aisle, as if they had touched some dangerous abyss and then taken a bit of it with them.

A shadow crept by across the shop's back wall. Someone was loitering outside the front windows.

The shop was closed. The sign on the door made that clear and she'd turned off half the lights as another big hint. If someone had any business with Charya, she didn't want to get caught up in it. She sidestepped behind some shelves of artifacts.

The door shook as the person outside tried to open it.

There, it's locked, Rose thought. *Now go away.*

Glass shattered at the front of the shop.

That was no customer at the front door. It was a thief. Rose was about to be trapped in the middle of a robbery.

She peered around the shelf to get a look at the front door. A burly man in Western clothes reached in through the broken glass and twisted the lock over to unlocked. The man certainly wasn't Cambodian. He would have looked at home in a rundown pool room or a gangster's getaway car. He kicked open the door.

Rose ducked back out of sight. She did not want to get involved with whatever this man was going to do. Her only hope was to get out the back door and hope that somehow she could find Rick and Charya when they got back.

She took a deep breath and then made a dash down the back aisle to the rear door.

"Hey you!"

The man had entered the shop and was already halfway to the exit Rose was counting on using.

Her foot slipped on the tile floor. She grabbed a table edge for balance.

That was all the delay the thief needed. He moved damn fast for a bulky guy. In a flash, he blocked the end of the aisle. Rose froze.

"Now there, Miss." His accent was British. "Where might you be off to in such a hurry?"

"Look, this isn't my store. Take whatever you want and leave. I don't want to be involved."

"Too late for that now." The man took a step toward her. "You got yourself involved when you decided to steal from Mr. Khong."

Rose caught her breath. This man was no thief. He was a thug working for Khong, and if he knew Rick and Charya were trying to get the jade hand, something bad had happened to the two of them. This thug had come here specifically for her.

The man flashed a malevolent smile and took another step closer. Rose's only hope was a desperate dash for the front door. She spun around and ran.

Before her second step, the thug was on her. He clamped his arms around her waist and pinned her arms to her sides. She screamed and tried to wriggle free. His arms felt like bands of iron.

"You Americans," he said. "Always thinking you're so superior. Well, you're about to learn that Mr. Khong is the wrong man to cross in Cambodia."

He started to drag Rose backward. She screamed for help.

The thug covered her mouth with one hand. "You think one of these locals will cross Mr. Khong to help you? Good luck with that."

His move only left his one arm around her waist. It still held her tight, but this was her chance.

She drove the heel of her foot down hard on top of his. His canvas shoe tore and bones crunched.

The thug cried out in pain and anger. His grip loosened.

Rose spun free. Beside her sat the open red box containing the powerful incense. She grabbed the box, held it in front of the man's face, and blew.

The thug's head went hazy in a rouge-infused cloud. He coughed and waved his hands in front of his face. Tears streamed from his eyes as he bent down and gagged.

Rose grabbed the biggest thing she could find, a stone statute about a foot high on a solid pedestal. She swung it hard and connected with the thug's temple. He moaned, wobbled, and then hit the floor. Blood seeped from a gash on his head.

Now Rose coughed. A bit of her incense attack had backfired. She wiped the dark dust from her face. The statue's base carried a splash of the thug's blood. She set it back on the table and wondered if she'd killed the man.

He was still breathing. While she didn't regret for a moment defending herself, and the man was clearly a lowlife, she was glad his death wouldn't be on her conscience.

But her relief was short-lived. Now she stood in a smashed shop in a foreign city where she did not speak the language. A criminal gang had her in its sights and another member might be right outside now. And for all she knew, those thugs already had Rick and Charya.

Her situation had gotten much worse.

CHAPTER TWELVE

Rick made a desperate grab for something, anything, along the *Mercury's* hull to keep him from being sucked into the stern. All he found was flat, cold steel.

The propwash pulled Rick off the stern and sucked him toward the starboard propeller. He twirled helplessly, head just above the water. He knew he was about to cash out of this game for good. His last thought was what would happen to Rose without him to look after her.

Far above, a load of cargo hit the deck with a crash like an avalanche. Some idiot had loaded too much too fast. The added weight sent the stern plunging into the river.

The props disappeared beneath the water.

Rick floated over the starboard prop. The rush of water underneath him ruffled his shredded shirt. He cleared the stern and could not believe his good luck.

The push of the propeller wash sent Rick downstream even faster. South of the dock, a string of rocks and boulders formed a breakwater that jutted into the river. With a few tired kicks of his legs, Rick managed to get to the part of the current that would take him there. In a few moments, he landed on one of the rocks.

He pulled himself up high enough to get his feet out of the water, but that was all the strength he had in him. He rolled to his back and collapsed.

He dreaded having to explain all of this to Rose. Once he figured out a way to get back to her, that was.

Headlights swept across the breakwater. Rick watched a truck turn onto the road along the riverbank. He recognized it as Charya's and a wave of relief swept over him. He raised a hand and waved.

The truck screeched to a halt at the end of the breakwater. Charya jumped out and began picking his way down the jumble of rocks.

"Rick! Are you hurt?"

Rick gave himself a once-over. "Bumps, bruises, and scrapes."

Rick stood up. Every part of his body hurt. He began an unsteady, lurching navigation of the breakwater rocks. He met Charya and the antiques dealer helped him back down the breakwater and into the truck.

"How did you get out?" Rick asked.

"I doubled back once the goons came after you. When I heard the gunshots and the splash, I was afraid what I'd find downstream was a floating corpse."

Rick slouched down in the seat. "No, I just feel dead."

Charya threw the truck into gear. "We need to get back to the shop. Khong's men know I was here. They will come looking for me."

Rick jerked back upright. "And they'll find Rose. Let's go!"

Charya hit the accelerator and headed back to the shop, dodging other vehicles and pedestrians the entire way. Still, Rick wished he'd drive faster.

They finally pulled up in front of the store. The door was open, the glass in it broken. Rick leapt from the truck in a panic. Charya was right behind him. The two burst into the store. The lights were out but the pale light from the street illuminated a wrecked shop.

"Rosie!" Rick called out. "Where are you?"

A light switch snapped on. Lights in the shop flickered. Rose stood at the rear door. She looked disheveled and stressed. Rick rushed to her and held her in his arms.

"I was afraid Khong's men had gotten you," he said.

"And I was worried they'd gotten you." She let go of Rick and gave him a gentle push away. She fingered his torn shirt. "Why are you soaking wet and smelling like a combination fish market/gas station?"

"Things went haywire at the warehouse. A bunch of Khong's thugs showed up."

"Same thing here."

Rose turned Rick around so he could face the last aisle in the shop. Broken artifacts littered the floor. The floor also hosted one of Khong's goons, unconscious, bloodied, and hog-tied.

"He broke in," Rose said, "then tried to kidnap me."

Rick smiled, wrapped an arm around Rose's waist, and gave her a squeeze. "When will men learn not to mess with my Rosie. I don't know why I worry about you."

Charya walked over to the man, knelt, and examined his oozing head wound. He ran his finger across the man's cheek and his fingertip came up coated with a fine powder.

"How did you do this to him?" Charya said.

"When he grabbed me, I blinded him with some incense, then clobbered him with a statue."

Charya examined the bloodied statue near the man. He grimaced.

"I'm sorry if the statue was rare," Rose said. "I just grabbed the closest thing."

Charya bounced up off the floor. "We need to get out of here now. As soon as this brute doesn't return, Khong's men will come looking for him."

"Where can we go?" Rick said.

"The men at the warehouse know what we look like," Charya said, "and this guy on the floor will remember Rose for sure. They will put the word out and anyone looking for a payday will turn us in. There won't be anywhere safe in the city."

"We can go back to the plane," Rose said. "It's outside the city, hidden, and we're the only ones who know it's there."

"Sounds like the best bet," Rick said. "And I could use a new shirt."

Charya seemed to be mulling the idea. "Okay. We go back to the plane."

CHAPTER THIRTEEN

Everyone was quiet during the ride back to the plane. Charya seemed focused on driving and going as fast as he could through the dark, unlit roads. Rose stared off out the window, though Rick was sure she couldn't see anything in the darkness any better than he could. Rick wanted to talk with her about how she was feeling after all the excitement back at the shop, but he had to wait until the two of them were alone. Rick guessed Rose wouldn't want to be that open in front of Charya. He knew he sure didn't.

After a while, the truck slowed and then turned right into a field.

"You'd better honk the horn," Rick said. "We don't want to startle Humphrey and have him start throwing tools at us."

The truck bumped along across the field. As it closed on the tree line, the headlights lit up the camouflaged shape of Humphrey's plane. Charya honked the horn twice. Just as they arrived at the plane, Humphrey staggered out from under a canvas-draped wing. He shaded his eyes from the headlights.

"It's us!" Rick called out.

Charya doused the lights and the field got very dark. Humphrey turned on a flashlight. Rick used it as a guide to lead everyone to the plane. As they passed under the canvas Rick noticed that the engine cowling was still open.

"Rick," Humphrey said, "glad you made it back, but hate to tell you that the plane ain't ready to leave yet."

"Neither are we." Rick gave Humphrey a quick rundown of the night's bad news, including Rose being attacked in Charya's shop.

"That's why we decided to come back and bunk in your plane," Rose said.

"Might as well," Humphrey said. "Until I fix the oil leak, that's about all she's good for."

The four entered the plane and took seats in the cabin. Humphrey lit a small lantern to give them light. Instead of providing comfort, it gave everyone a creepy, shadowy look.

Rose turned to Rick, "As soon as this bucket of bolts can get airborne, we're going home. No ifs-ands-or-buts. We came to sneak the jade hand out of a warehouse and that plan failed. Khong has the hand, his people are ruthless, and we are in way over our heads. We need to cut our losses."

Rick hated like hell to give up on the kind of payday that jade hand could deliver. But Rose was right. "Agreed. One thing I don't get is how there could be two jade hands?"

"That was troubling," Charya said. "Did they seem like a matched set?"

"Yep, one right, one left."

"I'm going to guess none of you know of King Jayavarman VII."

"He ruled Cambodia at the end of the 12th century," Rose said.

Charya's eyes went wide with shock. "Yes, he did."

"I researched this country before we left." She gave Rick a sharp look. "Since no one else was going to."

"I was very busy," Rick said.

"King Jayavarman VII ruled over a vast Cambodian empire," Rose said. "He had some sort of epiphany and decided to force all the citizens to abandon their Hindu religion for Buddhism. The rebellion against his edicts led to the eventual collapse of the empire."

"Very good, Rose," Charya said. "It was a savage, brutal time. Cities were consumed by bloodshed, abandoned, and lost to the jungle to this day. There was one city, soon known as Chraknorok, that turned to the Hindu god Rudra the Destroyer to bring them victory in battle."

"Not sure I'd ask for help from a god with 'destroyer' in its name," Humphrey said.

"That should tell you how desperate things had become for the leaders of Chraknorok. Rudra demanded rubies through which she could wield her power. The rulers forced anyone in the city who wasn't in the military into slavery as miners. The story is that they worked day and night, turning the ground under the city into a maze of mining tunnels as they searched for the perfect ruby."

"That's horrible," Rose said.

"Indeed. Chraknorok is a shortened version of what people began to call the city, *chrak tvear norok* in Khmer. What you would call 'the gate of hell'."

"Sounds like the king needed to capture that city," Rick said.

"And he embarked on a great march with thousands of soldiers into the jungle to do that. In order to summon Rudra permanently to our world, the Chraknorok rulers built a bigger than life-sized stone statue of the god, hand carved in exquisite detail, with jade hands. And in the center of its forehead was a massive ruby, called the Scarlet Heart of the Khmer. With that in place, the god could be summoned and directed to possess a human vessel. Once walking the Earth, there would be no stopping it.

"Confident that their god was about to deliver them victory, the Chraknorok troops left a minimal guard and joined the summoning ritual. Just as the priests were starting the final incantations, King Jayavarman VII attacked. The assault caught the rebels unaware. The king's troops overran them, stormed the main temple, and killed the designated woman just as Rudra was about to take her as its vessel.

"The rulers were slaughtered, the enslaved miners set free. To make sure no one could ever try summoning Rudra again, the king ordered the statue destroyed. But due to some enchantment, it could not be. The hands, carved separately, could be disassembled, but no amount of force could destroy them or the stone statue. So the king separated the hands from the body, and pried free the Scarlet Heart ruby. He then collapsed the entire mine and the buildings above it atop the body. All references to the city on maps and records were erased so it could never be found again."

"What about the hands and the ruby?" Rick said.

"The king dispersed the three separated items so they could be hidden forever. Three different men secreted an item each, and then committed suicide without telling the king or anyone else where the pieces had been hidden."

"And you think these were the Rudra statue's jade hands?" Rick said.

"Khong is a true believer in Rudra, believes that she can reduce the world to ash and then he can rebuild it to his twisted liking. Years ago, he financed a legitimate expedition to find Chraknorok. The expedition was supposedly lost in the jungle, though how such experts could ever be made no sense. The rumor was that they did find the lost city, and Khong murdered them all so only he knew the location."

"That sounds like the kind of guy who would want to reunite the statue, excavate the temple, and give resurrecting Rudra a second try," Rose said.

"If he has both hands, he'll need to find the Scarlet Heart ruby, unless he already has it," Rick said.

"There are a group of monks living in the mountainous region around Phenum Aoral," Charya said. "They claim to have the Scarlet Heart secure in a temple built into a hillside."

"Claim?"

"Their story is that bandits intercepted and killed the king's emissary carrying the ruby. But the gods intervened and sent a great storm against the bandits. All but one died horrible deaths. Rising waters and blocked roads rerouted the surviving bandit to the monastery. Realizing he must atone for his sins to be spared, he handed over the Scarlet Heart to the monks. The storm abated and he left in peace."

"The monks knew this ruby had more than just its value as a jewel?" Rick said.

"Absolutely. They took it as a sacred duty to keep it safe. They built a temple into a hillside as a kind of vault for it. It is said that since then they have guarded it around the clock."

"Sounds a little like one of my grandpa's tall tales," Humphrey said.

"It surely does. And that is why most disbelieve the story. But Khong will leave no stone unturned in his search. Raiding the monastery would become a big news story, so he'd hold off on that until he had all the other pieces in place. If he has the statue reassembled, he will start the search for the ruby right there."

"We need to warn the poor monks that Khong is coming," Rose said. "Give them a chance to hide themselves and the jewel somewhere else."

"Whoa," Rick said. "Didn't you just say we needed to get home because we were in over our heads?"

"And as soon as we warn the monks, that's just what we're doing. If you hadn't taken the jade hand, it would not have been in our shop to steal, and it wouldn't be in Khong's custody now. We, and by 'we' I mean Rick, got this avalanche of awful tumbling toward the monks, and the least we can do is warn them it's coming."

"I've never been to their monastery," Charya said, "and don't know anything more about them than what I've told you. Honestly, I only have a general idea where the place is, but if we leave now, we can be there early tomorrow. These goons here won't leave until late in the day if Khong is going to order them to get the ruby."

"It's our responsibility to try." Rose turned to Rick. "Isn't it?"

Rick knew when to fold a losing hand. "You got it, Rosie. Let's go."

CHAPTER FOURTEEN

After an hour or so of driving through the impenetrable blackness of the Cambodian countryside, dawn finally arrived. The sun rose over lush green fields of rice paddies interspersed with acres of regimented rows of plantation trees. Rose couldn't make out what types of trees they were. Tiny villages and single homes dotted the landscape. What she didn't see were the tractors and machinery so common on American farms.

Even this early in the day, some of the people who worked this land by hand were already toiling calf-deep in flooded rice paddies. They stood bent over as they pulled handfuls of unwanted volunteer plants from the water. Thatched, conical hats shielded their faces from the sun's rays as well as Rose's clear view. She wondered if they were young or old. She guessed this lifestyle would make the young people old before their time.

Every trip she and Rick took out of the country made her more appreciative of the life the two of them led.

The further they got from the city, the bumpier and narrower the road got. Based on the water buffalo and carts she saw in the villages, she figured that this road didn't see a lot of automobiles.

Rick and Charya had been taking turns driving. Right now, Rick sat beside her.

"Charya," Rick said, "what else do you know about these monks?"

"Very little. They have almost no contact with the rest of the world. Since they were entrusted with the Scarlet Heart, they have spent all their time and energy defending it."

"Isn't there some cardinal or bishop they report to like in other religions?"

"Buddhist monasteries are much more independent, each having its own rules. This one is the most independent. It was said that they even set aside many core teachings if they conflicted with the mission of keeping the Scarlet Heart safe. What we find at the monastery may have very few similarities to any monasteries I have visited."

"There seem to be more unknowns than knowns about what we are going to be stepping into," Rose said.

"It'll be okay, Rose," Rick said. "These monks will be glad we're giving them a heads-up about Khong."

Rose wondered if this was another example of Rick employing his "fake it 'till you figure it out" method of getting through life. She was afraid it was.

With the stress and excitement of the evening wearing off, exhaustion came upon Rose full force. The rising sun made it worse. Instead of rejuvenating her, it banished the dread she'd felt passing through the pitch-black night. She rested her head against Rick's shoulder.

"You were right to insist we warn these monks," he whispered to her.

She gave Rick's leg a pat. "You should use those first three words more often. They really suit you."

Rick gave her hand a squeeze. Rose sighed and fell asleep.

***

Rose stood alone in a small clearing in an Asian jungle. The sun beat down straight overhead from a clear blue sky. The air was so humid that she was bathed in sweat.

From the bushes in front of her, a woman emerged. She wore what looked like an Indian sari, finished in a pretty pattern of black and orange. Her long, black hair ran down past her shoulders and her face was pretty enough to be on a magazine cover. She walked toward Rose.

Rose tried to ask who she was, but she could not speak. In fact, she could not move at all. Rose stood frozen in place, not even blinking. She questioned whether she was breathing.

As the woman got closer, dread metastasized inside Rose. Everything about the woman appeared benevolent, but the closer she got, the more Rose sensed she was anything but.

"As it has been planned for so long," the woman said. "You are now ready."

Rose didn't know what the woman was talking about and was certain that she really didn't want to know.

The woman stopped before Rose and placed her hands against Rose's cheeks. The soft-looking hands felt scaly and hot.

"From the day you were born," she said, "I have seen you were destined for this moment."

A second set of arms appeared at the woman's sides. They reached up and the hands grabbed Rose's throat. They squeezed and Rose choked.

"There will be no stopping my return," she said.

The woman's skin turned a rich shade of blue. Her lips split into a malicious smile filled with sharp teeth. Panic boiled up inside Rose.

Rick came running from the jungle behind the woman. But as soon as he entered the clearing, he jerked to a stop, as if he'd hit an invisible wall. He pounded at it with his fists. He screamed Rose's name, but he didn't make a sound.

"No one can help you now," the woman said. "It is all ordained."

The blue-faced woman's eyes began to glow red. Then her mouth opened impossibly wide, and she swallowed Rose's head whole.

***

Rose snapped wide awake with her heart hammering in her chest. She was sitting in the truck and the sun's rays stabbed at her eyes as the vehicle bumped down the road. Her head rested on Rick's shoulder. He reached over and held her hand.

"Are you okay?" he said.

She felt confused. "Huh? Yes. I guess. I had a nightmare."

But as soon as she acknowledged the dream, the memory of it dissipated like morning fog in sunlight.

Rick wrapped his arm around her shoulders. "Just a dream. Everything's going to be fine."

She so wanted that to be true. She closed her eyes as her heart slowed down, and she nodded off.

***

"This is it," Charya said.

Charya stopped the truck short of a block stone wall at least six feet high. A square spire topped an arch over the road. Blotches of black mildew stained the stones and wild vines crisscrossed the wall. A polished, solid rosewood door filled the arch. The door had a rich, natural red, almost the color of blood. Rose knew buyers who would pay a fortune for something so rare.

An imposing, carved stone face glared down at the truck from the center of the arch. The weatherbeaten face had lost all its finer features, but the eyes had been spared that indignity and seemed to stare down at Rose. The carving looked familiar, but she could not place from where.

"In we go," Rick said.

74

Charya turned to Rose. "How are you feeling?"

Rose was taken aback. She hadn't complained about the journey, even though it had been trying and uncomfortable. "I'm fine."

Charya's eyes stayed on her for a moment, as if expecting more of an answer. Rose did not have anything else to add.

"She's tougher than she looks," Rick said.

"Let me go in first," Charya said. "Make sure the monks know we are no threat."

Rick looked wary. "No, let's all go."

"Absolutely," Rose said. "Charya, you can't think that I'm a flower ready to wilt in the heat *and* could be seen as a threat to these monks at the same time."

Charya seemed ready to protest but then thought better of it. The three of them left the truck and approached the door. A near-invisible main door within the larger door was a perfect match to the overall woodgrain. When they stopped in front of it, Rose noticed there was no knocker and also no handle or latch.

"It's like they don't want company," Rick said.

Charya raised his hand to knock, but before he could, the sound of wood scraping wood came from the other side, followed by a metallic clank. The smaller door opened to reveal a thin, young monk in a saffron-colored robe. Sweat glistened on his shaved head. He looked the three of them over through round, rimless glasses.

"Americans," he said with disdain. "We do not allow visitors."

"We aren't here to visit, but to warn," Charya said. "Dangerous men are coming for the Scarlet Heart of Khmer."

The monk looked them over again. "Your truck stays outside. I will take you to our abbot. He will decide."

The monk waved them in through the door. Once they were inside, he closed the door and replaced a heavy crossbeam that kept the door secure. Then the monk led them down a stone path.

Statues of stout, seated men with conical hats and bare chests lined both sides of the walkway. Patches of green fungus grew like a cancer on most of the statues and all were in disrepair. Some were missing limbs, others had faces scarred by the elements and missing noses or ears. Rose had the impression these were all carved centuries ago. Perhaps the skills to repair them no longer existed in the modern world, or at least the monks no longer possessed them.

On both sides of the path, other monks in matching saffron robes traversed the compound enclosed by the wall. Like the monk at the gate, all had shaved heads.

At the end of the path stood a stone building about a hundred feet wide. Three spires rose in the center. The middle one was thirty feet tall, with the two that flanked it being slightly shorter. The same face carved over the entrance gate was carved into the center spire. This version was better preserved and now Rose recognized it had adorned several incense burners back at the antiques shop.

An open doorway under the center spire had a pair of elephant heads carved to each side of it. Like the statues, this building had seen the ravages of time. All adorning details of its design were gone, replaced by crumbling stone surfaces. Piles of the molted remains lay against the side of the building.

The monk led them through the entrance and into a surprisingly well-maintained room. A tiled floor shined as if recently waxed. Candles burned in gold-leafed sconces on the walls. In the center, a monk sat closed-eyed in contemplation on a gold chair with a red velvet cushion. This monk wore a purple sash around his waist.

The monk approached the man on the chair and touched his arm. The man's eyes opened.

"Abbot Dara," the monk whispered, "these people have worrisome news for you."

The abbot waved them forward. Charya led the way. They stopped before the abbot.

"Abbott," Charya said. "I am Charya Thang and this is Rick and Rose Sinclair from America."

"We are a contemplative order," Abbot Dara said. "We neither encourage nor welcome visitors."

"We would not interrupt if it wasn't important. Some very dangerous men are on their way here to steal the Scarlet Heart of Khmer."

The placid look on the abbot's face did not change. "You should not be concerned. The Scarlet Heart is safe, as it always has been and always will be."

"Sir," Rick said. "You don't understand. These men were sent by Rathanak Khong."

"We live a secluded life here. His name means nothing to me."

"Well, it's going to mean something soon. We already had a few run-ins with his thugs and they are ruthless."

"All over Cambodia there are jewels of greater value that are easier to steal," the abbot said. "Why would he make such a great effort now to take something guarded here for centuries?"

"We think he has reassembled the statue of Rudra the Destroyer from Chraknorok," Rose said. "All he needs is the Scarlet Heart to complete it."

Dara closed his eyes and bowed his head. After a deep breath, he opened his eyes and looked at the three.

"Prophesy has forewarned us that this would happen," Dara said. "So we have remained prepared for it. Our monks pray and meditate daily. They spiritually strong and that power will keep the Scarlet Heart safe."

Rose wasn't one to criticize someone's faith in whatever religion they wanted to practice. But if this abbot thought spiritual strength could deflect bullets, he was going to lead his monks to early graves.

"And the Scarlet Heart is in its guarded shrine, a veritable fortress built into the hillside. Quite impenetrable."

"I know you don't get out much," Rick said, "but there was a world-wide war a few years back and explosives know-how has gotten much better since this monastery was built. Nothing is impregnable."

"I will show you to allay your fears. And then you all must go. Your presence is a disruptive wind affecting the monks' meditation."

"If he thinks we're a disruptive wind," Rose whispered to Rick, "Khong's men will be a hurricane."

Dara stopped in his tracks as he walked past them. He turned to Rose. "Your spirit is distressed."

"I think we all are," Rose said.

"No, something else…deeper."

Rose was confused, and a little insulted. "I don't know what you mean."

"Wait here."

The abbot entered a room off the main chamber and returned moments later. He carried a rosewood disc about three inches across and a quarter inch thick. He handed it to Rose. "This will help you."

Rick stepped up beside Rose and they looked at the piece. On one side was carved what looked like a ship's wheel, with eight spokes and an ornate center. Rose flipped it over and the reverse had a diamond-shaped design of intertwined lines that met at right angles. They twisted from above and beneath each other with no beginning or end. They made a gorgeous geometric pattern.

Rose sniffed it. "It smells like myrrh."

Before Rose could ask why he'd given her the disc, Dara left the building with Charya right behind him. Rose gave Rick a quizzical look.

Rick shrugged. "Maybe they give away souvenirs."

The two followed as Dara led the group out and across the compound. They passed a gaggle of seven monks sitting cross-legged in the shade of a large tree. Their eyes were closed, their hands on their knees. One monk struck what looked like a tiny gong. It sent out a single note. The group responded by humming a similar note.

"Khong doesn't need to send an army to wipe these people out," Rick said to Rose. "One man with a pistol should be plenty."

Soon they approached a hillside. A ten-foot-high stone edifice jutted from the vine-covered ground. Its blocks were three feet long and two feet high. Unlike the rest of the monastery, these stones weren't coated in black mold and were completely intact.

"That is the Shrine of the Scarlet Heart of Khmer," the abbot said. "A monk within prays and guards the ruby every hour of the day."

"Khong's men will force the door and kill the monk," Charya said.

"There is no door to force."

"How do your monks get in and out?" Rose said.

"They do not. They only go in. Blocks are removed from the wall, a monk enters, the wall is re-sealed."

"How long does the monk stay within the shrine?"

"Until he dies."

"That won't take long starving to death in there," Rick said.

Dara pointed to a smaller brick in the face of the wall. "That stone is removed daily to deliver food and clean clothing. An underground stream provides water and takes away waste. The occupant leads a long and fulfilling life in the presence of the Scarlet Heart."

Rose wasn't sure how being in solitary confinement with a gemstone could be a fulfilling experience.

"Dara," Rick said. "Explosives leveled buildings thicker and taller than that in the Great War. It isn't still 900 A.D."

From the main gate area came the shrill bleat of some kind of horn. It paused and repeated. Dara whirled around to face in that direction. Then came the sound of gunshots.

Rose's heart skipped a beat. It seemed their warning had been delivered too late.

CHAPTER FIFTEEN

Back at the plane, Humphrey lamented agreeing to join this journey to the wrong side of the world.

He stood under the wing and looked up into the open #3 engine cowling. His plane wasn't going anywhere, and neither were he and the Sinclairs, if he didn't get the oil leak under control.

If this had happened at home, it would not have been a problem. The Ford Tri-motor had common enough engines and he could find the gasket he needed. But he was not at home. He was in the jungle countryside of a French colony. There was no sign of nearby civilization, and even if there was, the French he'd mastered during his war years in Europe was only good for ordering liquor.

He'd spent plenty of time in the Okefenokee Swamps in Georgia, but this place really gave him the willies. The whooping, screeching animal noises emanating from the forest sounded like nothing he'd ever heard before. The insects seemed to all come in the twice-Georgia-size variety. The humid air felt thick enough to choke him and there was a stench from the jungle he was sure even vultures would turn their beaks up at.

On top of all this, he and his plane had no legal standing to be here. He'd flown in without permission, avoiding customs and border patrol, and plopped down somewhere that definitely wasn't an airport. His experiences skirting export regulations around the world had taught him that colonial officials of any European empire were uniformly petty, greedy, and corrupt. He was certain that at any moment, some small Frenchman in a pith helmet was going to tromp across the field with colonial soldiers at his side. The man's first action would be to lock up Humphrey's plane. His second action would be to lock up Humphrey.

That scenario meant Humphrey couldn't leave his plane to hike into Phnom Penh on the million-to-one shot they had an open aircraft parts store. He was going to have to see what he had onboard to get his plane back in the air.

He went back to the cabin door and stepped up into the aircraft. He hung his new hat on the door latch and went to the rear of the plane. He kept a variety of tools and odds and ends on board for emergencies such as this. But it was more of a pack rat's collection than some kind of formal emergency kit. He wasn't sure what he had onboard, but he was about to find out.

He opened the door to the storage area in the rear bulkhead. The first thing he saw was no help at all. A newspaper sat on the deck. He'd planned on reading it while waiting for Rick and Rose to arrive at the airfield near Savannah. There hadn't been time for that then, and there sure wasn't now. He picked it up. The banner for the Savannah Evening Press made him even more homesick. He tossed the paper aside in the cabin.

Humphrey grabbed a crate from the space and moved it to the cabin floor. The jumble of tools, parts, and materials made it look more like a full trash bin than a mechanic's tool chest. He began to empty it item by item and lay the contents on the cabin floor.

Minutes later he had an array of tools (several broken), replacement parts (none he needed), lengths of control cables (he did not recognize), and a trio of packaged greases and sealants (all dried out and rock hard).

"Dang," Humphrey said. "Might have been a good idea to look this mess over *before* the trip instead of during."

He went to put a wrench back in the crate when he noticed something lining the bottom. His eyes lit up. He reached in and tucked one fingernail under the corner. Then with the reverence a curator reserves for priceless art, he gently peeled the liner up and held it in the light.

"Well, ain't you sweeter than fresh honey?"

It wasn't a liner. It was a rectangle of gasket material. He wasn't sharp enough to remember putting it in there, but thank the Lord that at some point, he'd been sharp enough to think tucking it into the crate would be a good idea.

He set the gasket material on the cabin floor. A chattering noise came from the cabin doorway. He looked up to see a two-foot-tall brown monkey standing there. A tail at least as long as its body curled at its feet. A darker brown stripe ran across the top of its head. It had a gaunt, fleshy face like a wizened old man with muttonchops and a set of green-gold eyes that made Humphrey shiver.

It screeched and displayed a nasty looking set of yellowed teeth. The sound echoed inside the aircraft. Then the monkey grabbed Humphrey's hat from the door latch and bolted from the plane.

"My new hat! You get back here!"

Humphrey scrambled up off his knees and over to the door, kicking tools aside as he did. At the doorway, he paused and looked out across the open area for the monkey. It stood in the field about fifty yards away, with Humphrey's hat in its hand, looking like a kid holding his father's cap for him.

After all Humphrey had gone through to get that hat, he wasn't going to let some damn ape swipe it. He jumped to the ground, and sprinted for the monkey.

The creature didn't run, didn't even seem concerned. It just stared Humphrey down as he closed on it.

Humphrey planned to throttle that little thief to within an inch of its life when he caught it.

Just as Humphrey closed to within a few yards of the monkey, it made a noise that sounded far too much like a laugh. Then it whirled like a discus thrower and sent the saucer cap sailing through the air further out into the field. Then the monkey sprinted in the opposite direction for the jungle.

Humphrey cursed and went for his hat. He arrived to find it sticking out of the spongy ground by the brim. He plucked it up by the headband and flicked the mud from the brim with one finger. An inspection revealed no harm had been done. He exhaled, set the hat on his head, and adjusted it to a bit of a rakish angle. With a satisfied smile on his face, he turned back to his plane.

His jaw dropped.

A squad of monkeys ran in and out of his plane through the cabin door. The outbound monkeys were carrying things and heading for the jungle.

"Hell, no!" Humphrey ran back to the plane. Before he was halfway there, the last of the monkeys jumped from the cabin and beat a retreat among the trees.

Humphrey climbed into the plane. The cabin smelled like the wrong end of a circus tent. Half the tools he'd taken from the crate were gone. His heart sank as he saw that so was the sheet of gasket material.

Those monkeys had just cost him his airplane.

CHAPTER SIXTEEN

This dangerous situation had been Rick's worst fear when he'd seen these scrawny, unarmed monks. Khong's men had arrived before he and Rose could leave. Now they were about to be on the wrong end of a one-way gunfight.

He turned to Charya. "How could Khong's men get here so quickly?"

"Maybe this is another gang that was waiting nearby for word that the jade hands were in Khong's possession."

"Take refuge in the nearest building," Dara said. "I must lead the monks' defense."

The abbot sprinted back in the direction of the main temple with his robe flapping behind him like a cape. Rick was surprised that an older man who he'd only seen move slowly and serenely could run like an Olympian. Maybe there was more to the monks' regimen than just mental meditation.

From behind them came the sound of grinding stone. Rick turned around just as the access brick in the shrine wall was pushed out. It fell and hit the ground with a thud. A rifle barrel poked out of the opening.

"The ruby's guard is armed!" Rose said.

"He won't go down without a fight," Charya said, "and we don't want to be in that crossfire."

Rick grabbed Rose's hand and then pointed to the nearest structure. It was a patio enclosed by a four-foot stone wall and covered by a thatched roof. "Let's go. That's our first stop."

The three ran for the patio. More gunshots rang out from the main gate area. Rick held Rose's hand tighter. The group entered the patio. It contained a scattering of chairs and tables atop a dirt floor. Rick and Rose dove for the shelter of the far wall, Charya for the side wall. Rose missed her step and tumbled in against the stone blocks.

"Are you okay?" Rick said.

Rose rubbed her knee and winced. "Just a scrape, I think. Hey, sorry I got us into this fix. Charya promised we'd be away before anyone got here."

"I'm the one who agreed to the abbot's tour," Rick said. "We should have left right away. There's enough blame to go around. We'll get out of this okay. Trust me."

Rick flashed his most charming smile. Rose did not smile back.

Rick peeked over the top of the wall. He had a good view of the grounds and the main gate beyond. Rushing monks swarmed across the compound. To Rick's surprise, they carried rifles.

"You sure this is a monastery and not a military post?" Rick said to Charya.

"It's not a normal monastery. I've never seen a Buddhist monk with any kind of weapon. As I said, this is a different kind of sect here."

Sustained gunfire penetrated the rosewood gate door. A monk behind it cried out and dropped to the ground. Then a heavy-duty truck burst through the arch, shattering the door. The truck bounced over the dead monk and landed on a section of the door. It caught in the suspension and the vehicle careened off to the right. It flattened two of the statues that lined the path, then struck a tree head on. The hood folded into a U. The driver's head slammed into the windshield and he went still. Steam billowed from the truck's nose.

Rick breathed a sigh of relief. But that respite was short-lived. Men armed with pistols and rifles tumbled out of the covered back of the truck. A second vehicle followed on the heels of the first. It avoided the debris and drove halfway up to the temple. Brakes screeched and the truck jerked to a stop. More armed men piled out of the back of this truck. They were more of Khong's recruited Western ex-patriate army. One of them carried a Tommy gun.

Rick guessed there were about a dozen overall. That was good news, because he'd seen more than twice that many monks, and since the alarm had sounded, every one he'd seen had been armed with a rifle.

Dara emerged from the temple and shouted orders to the monks. They formed a rough skirmish line between the intruders and the ruby's blockhouse shrine. They let loose a fusillade all along the line. Bullets sang off of the lead truck. Thugs screamed and dropped.

The rest of the crew scattered for cover. It seemed that their bravado had been fueled by the assumption they were doing their usual, preying on the defenseless.

A smattering of return fire from the thugs came the monks' way. None were hit and all kept shooting.

The Tommy gunner made his move. He darted out from behind one truck and sent a spray of rounds in the temple's direction. Bullets struck the earth in a line at the monks' feet. The gunner adjusted his aim and walked several rounds into one monk's chest. Blood exploded from his saffron robe. He fell back and hit the ground.

The rest of the monks shifted their aim to the gunner. In a second, bullets riddled the thug's body. His gun flew from his hands as he executed a spastic dance before a bullet struck his head and sent him down for good.

Two more monks were wounded and beat a retreat to safer ground. But Khong's men were getting the worst of it. Those who were not dead were pinned down and most of their shots poorly aimed. If Rick had been betting on this fight this morning, he'd have given 100-to-1 that the monks would last five minutes. He'd have lost that bet.

These thugs looked like they were about to throw in the towel.

Then a man exited the passenger seat of the lead truck. He wore a long, black robe. On the front was a white symbol that looked like an inverted Y with an angled crossbar halfway up the vertical. His black hair was tied in a topknot like a sumo wrestler and he was almost big enough to be one. His swarthy skin carried dozens of pockmark scars.

Dara shouted some kind of curse and pointed at the man in black. Between that and him being the only target standing in the open, the monks redirected their fire at him. But not one bullet found its mark. A slight haze surrounded the black-robed man, like the shimmer off an asphalt road on a hot day. Whatever that was had to be deflecting or stopping the bullets. At this distance, Rick could not be sure which. What he *was* sure of was that Topknot Man wasn't even flinching.

The man knelt, raised one fist, and brought it down knuckles-first to the ground. When he struck it, a semicircle of earth rose before him and swept outward, like a ripple in a pond. But unlike a ripple, as it expanded outward this wave strengthened instead of dissipated. The earth swelled until it crested at a six-foot wave before the line of monks.

It seemed that no amount of mental training could prepare the monks for this bizarre attack. The line broke and men fled in panic. But there was no escape. The cresting wave of earth came down on them like an avalanche. Dirt muffled the monks' terrified cries. Bodies crushed. Lives snuffed out.

The wave caught Dara differently and sent him cartwheeling across the compound. He struck a tree and lay still.

The wave may have crested but it did not disappear. It kept rolling outward as it spent its energy. It rolled under the main temple at three feet high. The temple's foundation rose and fell like a cracking whip. As it did, the outer towers folded in on the center one and all three came raining down. The stones within the walls split. The great face above the doorway came free, fell to the ground, and shattered into a hundred pieces.

The wave emerged at two feet tall on the temple's near side. In seconds it would hit their patio.

There was no time to run.

"Get down, Rosie!"

Rose ducked and Rick covered her head and shoulders with his body. He prayed they'd survive.

CHAPTER SEVENTEEN

The wave struck and felt like an earthquake. Sensing the always-solid ground turn to gelatin terrified Rick. The earthen floor rose and liquified. The thatch roof snapped and blew away. With their foundation gone, the walls crumbled. Stone blocks tumbled inward, trapping Rick, Rose and Charya underneath. Clouds of stone dust filled the air.

As soon as everything stopped moving, Rick tried to rise off of Rose before he suffocated her. The combined mass of several blocks threatened to pin his shoulders down forever. He strained against the weight. One block rolled away, then another. He pushed his chest off Rose. She coughed, drew in a deep breath, then coughed again.

"You okay, Rosie?"

Rose spit dirt from her lips. "I feel buried, but not broken. You?"

Rick gave himself a mental once over. "The same, I think. We're lucky a lot of the walls toppled and rolled over us instead of falling like the temple did."

Beside them, Charya lay unconscious and mostly buried, with just his head and one arm exposed. Blood seeped from a wound on his forehead. A cloud of dust billowed off a rock when he exhaled, so Rick knew he was at least alive.

Rick and Rose wriggled and shoved their way from under the fallen wall.

Rose checked the compound and then gripped Rick's arm. "Rick, they're coming."

Rick froze and looked across the compound. Topknot Man was leading his once-again fearless gang of goons across the grounds. But they weren't heading toward Rick and Rose. No one even seemed aware the two of them were there. The gang was making a beeline for the ruby's vault.

From the vault opening, the guardian's rifle fired. The bolt cycled and clinked and the rifle and another sharp report followed. Topknot Man raised one hand and a shield of distortion formed before him as he walked. At this range, Rick could actually see the bullet hit the shimmering air, stop cold, and drop to the ground.

The surviving thugs all opened fire at the vault. Bullets sent up spurts of dust as they slammed into stone around the opening. One or more found their mark. The guardian cried out and the rifle barrel retreated into the vault.

Topknot marched straight for the slit. The goons held back, displaying fearful looks. Topknot stopped several feet from the vault wall. He closed his eyes and raised both hands palms out toward the stone face.

Twin spirals of distortion shot from his palms. They hit the wall and blasted it to smithereens. The force blew all the debris inward and the new opening belched clouds of dust in return. Rick thought that if the bullets hadn't killed the ruby's companion, that blast surely had.

Beyond the opening lay only darkness. Topknot Man dashed in. Moments later he returned. He raised one hand to the sun. Between his thumb and forefinger he held the four-inch long Scarlet Heart of the Khmer. Sunlight struck it and it sent shafts of red light in all directions.

Rick and Rose gasped in unison at the sight.

Rick thought the crew might cheer at the sight of their leader holding their objective. But they did not. Instead, they just looked relieved, as if Topknot Man's punishment for failure would have been worse than facing the firing squad of monks they'd encountered.

Topknot Man clenched a fist around the ruby and began to walk back to the truck. He suddenly stopped.

Confusion crossed his face. He turned and faced Rick and Rose's hiding spot.

"He couldn't have heard us," Rose whispered.

She was right. And they hadn't moved a muscle to attract anyone's attention. Somehow Topknot Man had sensed them. He headed straight for them, with the thugs right behind him.

Rick's heart sank. They were both half-buried in stone blocks. They weren't going anywhere.

The group stopped just short of the fallen patio wall. Rick adopted a defiant look. They might be doomed, but that was just the kind of situation that demanded he "fake it until he figured it out."

But Topknot Man didn't even glance at Rick. Instead, he stared transfixed at Rose. He mumbled something in Cambodian Rick didn't understand. Then he turned to the thug beside him.

"She has been prepared for Rudra. The god's reach is greater than even I imagined, delivering her to us. Seize her. Bring her back to Chraknorok unharmed."

Three men scrambled over the debris and made rough work of uncovering Rose.

"Rick, help!" she cried out.

"Leave her alone!" Rick said. "Take me instead. I'll go without a fight."

Rose wasn't about to be that docile. As soon as the men freed her from the pile, she squirmed and tried to writhe free. But they were too big and too many. They grabbed her under the arms and lifted her off the ground. She kicked uselessly at the air.

Rick pushed up hard. More stones rolled off his back and buttocks. He was almost free.

"Let her go or I swear I will kill every one of you."

A thug to the leader's left laughed and stepped over to Rick. He sent one booted foot against Rick's head and Rick's world turned black.

***

Rick awakened to a massive headache and strained neck muscles. Face down on one of the stones, he sucked in a lungful of dust and choked. The moment he oriented himself, terror ripped through him.

Rose was gone.

He'd freed himself enough to rise to his knees. His head swam and he almost collapsed. But he steadied himself and surveyed the compound. A few surviving, half-buried monks moaned within the compound. What wasn't in the compound was the lead truck, any of the gangsters, or his beautiful wife.

Charya moaned Rick's name. Rick crawled out from under the remaining blocks and over to Charya's side. He touched the man's arm and Charya's eyes fluttered open.

"You're alive," he managed to say. "And Rose?"

"Alive, but they kidnapped her and escaped with the Scarlet Heart."

Charya grimaced. "Get me out from under all this."

Rick carefully removed the rubble that pinned Charya down, then helped him sit up. Charya wiped the dust from his face.

"Anything broken?" Rick said.

"I think the block that grazed my head did the most damage, but I bet I look like an overripe banana under these clothes. Why did they take Rose and not you and I?"

"The leader said she had been prepared for Rudra, whatever that meant."

Charya's face fell. He looked across the compound. "We need to find Dara. Pray that he's alive."

Rick helped Charya to his feet. After a wobbly start, he waved Rick off. The two climbed out of the ruins and crossed the compound. The earth looked like a tiller had ripped through it. Over to the far left, two monks were digging a third out of the dirt. Whether he was alive or not Rick could not tell.

The tree Dara had struck stood cocked at an odd angle with many exposed roots. Dara was indeed alive, sitting up against the trunk. Dried blood scabbed the side of his bald head and his neck.

As the two approached, Dara stood up, using his left arm for support. His right arm hung limp at his side. He leaned against the tree, taking deep breaths.

"Praise all that is holy," Charya said, "you survived."

Dara cast a rueful look across the compound. "But most of my monks did not. I failed them. Even now, I have yet to help even one of the poor survivors or offer a prayer over the dead." He gave his right arm a swing. "This was dislocated. I popped it back. I think."

Rick had dislocated a shoulder once. The pain had been excruciating, especially when the doctor put it back into place. He couldn't imagine the little abbot smacking his shoulder back into its socket by himself. Just like Rose, he was tougher than he looked.

"I saw those men kidnap your wife," Dara said.

"And I'm going to get her back," Rick said. "The leader with the topknot said she had been prepared for Rudra. Who was he and what does that mean?"

"That man was Tiang Sangha." Dara sighed. "Once he was a monk here. I passed him over for another to become the Scarlet Heart's companion. His obsession with the stone seemed…unhealthy, his questions about it focused on its power. Of all the monks, he was the only one who begged to see it, to verify that it truly was within the shrine. He did not have the constitution for the responsibility of being its companion. Before dawn the day after I passed him over, he walked out of the front gate and disappeared."

"It looks like his next employer was Khong," Charya said.

"The garment he wore was of a high priest of Rudra the Destroyer. He has taken what he had learned here, and perverted it to be used for evil. If the statue body was still in the city Khong found, and Khong has both hands, as soon as that ruby arrives, Tiang will be able to call forth Rudra, and that will be catastrophic."

"Tiang didn't see Rose and I as much as sensed us," Rick said. "Or more likely sensed just her. He came straight for Rose. What did he mean when he said Rose had been prepared for Rudra?"

"He could not have been right about that," Dara said.

"Yes, he could," Charya said.

"What are you two talking about?" Rick said.

"Rudra cannot be brought into the corporeal world as she is," Dara said. "She must possess a human host. That host must be cleansed and consecrated in a ritual using the fresh blood of an enemy, an icon of Rudra, and a rare incense."

"And I think that happened," Charya said. "Back in my shop she was attacked by one of Khong's men. She defeated him by bashing him with a Rudra statue and overturned some incense containers in the process. The ritual incense was in one of those boxes."

Dara's eyes narrowed. "You fool. Why would you traffic in such a dangerous thing?"

"Because I sell what people want to buy. And until now, I considered all of this Rudra worship hokey nonsense."

"And now my wife has been kidnapped because of it," Rick said. "Fantastic."

"Then it is possible that she was inadvertently prepared for possession," Dara said, "or close enough to it that Tiang could sense that she was. When they get her to the lost temple city, they will try to bring Rudra into her."

"And if she wasn't properly prepared," Rick said, "it won't work?"

"Yes, but the process will kill her."

"That might be better than being possessed by some vengeful god," Rick said, "but I don't want either to happen. We need to find the lost temple city."

He had no idea how to do that. But he bet the driver of that wrecked truck had known.

He trotted over to the still steaming wreck. He opened the door and pulled the lifeless body from the driver's seat. A quick search uncovered a map with both this temple, Khong's rediscovered city, and a well-marked route between the two. The city was on the other side of some mountains. He brought the map back to the others and showed it to them.

"We know where they're going," Rick said.

"And that is a difficult route they are taking," Charya said. "Steep elevation changes and poor roads. It will take them days."

"Which was why Khong had them waiting nearby to strike as soon as he had the hands," Dara said.

"If we follow them, we'll be behind them the whole time," Rick said.

"Way behind," Charya said. "My truck can't manage those mountains."

"We need to get there first."

Charya pointed to a spot further east on the map. "We can travel east across the plains to the Mekong, and take the river up around the mountains, then come up on the lost city from the east. I think we'll get there first."

"I'll get the truck," Rick said.

"I'm coming with you," Dara said. "The Scarlet Heart is still my responsibility and I must get it back."

"You are in no condition," Charya said.

"And the two of you are walking blind into aspects of the supernatural you don't understand. You will need me."

Rick thought the old man had a point there. "We need to fashion a sling for your arm if you're going to travel."

The abbot untied the purple sash around his waist with his left hand. He passed it to Charya. "Use this. I don't deserve to wear the abbot's sash at this point."

Charya helped bind up Dara's arm and then the three headed for the truck. When they arrived, Rick entered through the passenger door and noticed Rose's handkerchief on the floorboard. He picked it up, placed it under his nose, and inhaled. Her scent made his nose tingle.

He gripped the handkerchief tightly.

"I will bring you home, Rosie," he whispered.

CHAPTER EIGHTEEN

Rose sat in the thugs' truck wedged between the driver and the group's leader with the topknot. The ride was rough, the seats unsupportive, and the stench of the two men unfit even for a barnyard.

But she was still better off than riding in the back. The surviving thugs from two trucks were crammed into one and that would have been worse. The leader's orders that Rose remain "alive and uninjured" had gotten her safely to the truck, but given the lecherous looks of some of the goons back there, she wasn't going to bet her life on that continuing.

She was only slightly less worried about her safety in the front seat. The leader had some kind of extraordinary power he'd used to kill the monks and destroy the shrine and temple. Based on the fear he inspired in his men, they'd likely seen him do more. Rose could sense evil boiling inside the man.

She decided this was one of her husband's "fake it until you figure it out" moments. A brave face would prove she wasn't another cowering female, and that might be a good start. She swept her hair from her face and took a deep breath.

"Your English is quite good, Mr. Khong," she said.

The man laughed. "I'm not Khong. I am Tiang Sangha. Only someone who knows neither of us could confuse us. And only someone who knows neither of us would try and get in the way of our plan. And I'm forced to speak this good English since Khong sucks up the dregs of the British Empire to fill his ranks."

Rose decided to throw a dart, test the thickness of Tiang's skin. "So, you are just one of the gang then?"

"Hardly. I am the High Priest of Rudra the Destroyer. She has gifted me the ability to channel her power in her service. And the monastery now lays in ruins as a result. Soon I will leverage that power to guide her passage from her prison world to ours, where she will make us kings in thanks for our service."

"I've heard the myth about her earlier failed attempt at crossing over."

"An unforeseen element delayed her passage, then the intervening army of King Jayavarman VII disrupted the rest of the ritual. None of that will happen again. Our location is secure, our threats eliminated, and this time Rudra's vessel is perfect."

"You think pretty highly of yourself to say you're perfect."

"Me? I'm not the vessel. You are."

Rose caught her breath. "I would never consent to that."

"Your consent is immaterial. You have been prepared for Rudra already. You will not be able to fight the power of a god."

"You said that before, that I was prepared. Nothing like that has happened to me. Until now, I hadn't even heard of Rudra."

That last part was a lie, but she forgave herself.

"Knowledge of or faith in Rudra is not necessary to become her vessel. You only need to be sanctified. And I can sense that you have been. You have undergone the *kalishan*, been anointed with the holy essences mixed with the blood of a vanquished enemy."

Rose was about to tell Tiang he needed to check his occult acts detector because it was way out of calibration. She hadn't vanquished an—

Then she remembered the thug she clobbered in the antiques shop, the one whose blood splashed on her.

"What are the holy essences?" she asked.

"A combination of incense, animal extracts, and powdered minerals. Your consciousness still reeks of it."

"That can't be valid. I wasn't even thinking then, just reacting. I was trying to stay alive, not trying to be cleansed."

"You do not choose to be cleansed. Rudra chooses you to be cleansed. Her reach is infinite. You do not belong on this side of the world, American, and yet you are here. You know almost nothing about our culture, yet you are about to become a central figure in it. How much of this did you choose?"

Rose flashed through the events of the last few days. Matty delivering the jade hand. Humphrey getting the shipping information. Humphrey's plane holding together long enough to land and not one second more. The thug finding her alone in the antique store. Even Rick couldn't rationalize the luck it would have taken for all of these events to happen, and all of them propel her here.

"I'll die before I let Rudra the Destroyer free."

"Oh no you won't. Rudra will make certain of that. You think you can stand tall against the power of a god?"

Her prospects didn't seem good for that.

"And now for an added layer of protection." Tiang pulled a long strip of cloth from his pocket. "I'm blindfolding you. Resist it, and the two of us will blindfold you *and* stuff a gag in your mouth. I think breathing this hot, humid air is already difficult enough without having it filtered through a dirty wad of cloth."

Rose submitted to the blindfold and then slumped down in her seat. She'd faked it until she figured it out, but now wished she hadn't figured it out at all. She was all alone facing a ruthless criminal gang and a god bent on her destruction.

She hoped Rick was hot on her trail with a damn good rescue plan.

***

Rick had to admit he had no rescue plan.

The multi-hour drive to the Mekong had given him plenty of time to devise one, but he'd come up with nothing. He only had one bit of information, the location of Chraknorok. He had no idea if he'd find Khong alone there in his lair, or surrounded by a thousand of his mercenary thugs. Would it be a single temple like the monastery they'd just left, or a sprawling compound? And once there, how would he ever find Rose?

All of it was more than he could worry about now. The only thing certain was that getting to Chraknorok was his only hope of rescuing his wife. This time, "leap before looking" was his only choice.

Rick could smell the Mekong before he saw it, and that smell was not good. The slow-moving rivers around Savannah got pretty rank at the peak of summer, and this scent put all of them to shame. Charya turned off the main road to a narrow dirt path that passed through thick stands of bamboo. After a slow mile of progress, they came to a wood and thatch shack on stilts at the river's edge. The Mekong itself flowed slow, wide, and muddy beyond it. What looked like two over-sized wooden canoes lay beached on the sand and tied off to one of the shack's stilts.

Charya stopped the truck by the steps up to the shack. Without the artificial breeze created by motion, the humid air seemed to thicken and threaten suffocation. A mosquito buzzed at Rick's ear.

"The man here is named Guo," Charya said. "He gets things up and down the river without delay and without raising suspicions."

"His business sounds unsavory," Dara said.

"I'm afraid the task we have to do is unsavory," Charya said, "so he is just our man. He's part of a network of smugglers running trade from China all the way to southern Vietnam. I will negotiate our passage. Come."

Charya led them up the few steps to the shack's open door. Inside at a bamboo table sat an obese Chinese man. The sides of his head were shaved, but the remaining stripe of hair trailed down his neck in a long braid. He glared at the doorway with small, black eyes recessed above puffy cheeks. Between those and his wide, slightly upturned nose, Rick could not help being reminded of a pig.

"Charya." Guo practically spat out the greeting. Then he reached under the table, pulled out a pistol, and set it on the table with a bang. The barrel pointed at the three of them. "You would be the last person I'd expect at my doorway."

Rick gritted his teeth. This wasn't the heartfelt welcome he'd expected. This was the kind of welcome that led to bloodshed.

"Unless I'd come to make amends," Charya said. "Let me introduce my associates, Abbot Dara and Rick Sinclair."

Guo looked at them as if just realizing there were two others in the door. He gave Dara a hard, dismissive look. "Traveling with a crippled monk, now, to make yourself seem holier?"

Charya smiled. "I'm too far gone for that."

"And this other is British?"

"American," Rick said.

"You're a long way from home, Yankee Doodle." Guo turned back to Charya. "Have your friends leave so the two of us can settle our differences without witnesses."

"These gentlemen are why I'm here. We need passage up the Mekong."

"Take a passenger boat. There are plenty."

"Not to where we are going. We're going to Chraknorok."

Guo leaned forward. "Khong never found Chraknorok, but you did?"

"Khong did find it. That's how I know where it is."

"Khong must still be there then," Guo said. "And you must have a death wish."

"We're going because he kidnapped my wife," Rick said. "And I want her back."

"And he stole an artifact from my temple," Dara said. "And I want that back."

"And what's in it for me to take you upriver?"

"Two things," Charya said.

He reached into his pocket and pulled out a roll of cash. He peeled off a half dozen bills from the outside of the roll and set them on the table.

"A fifty percent upfront to set out, the other fifty percent when we return. You can see I have it. But the real prize is I will confirm the city's location to you, and you alone. You remember what Chraknorok was?"

"A ruby mine."

"*The* ruby mine. And a mine in search of only the Scarlet Heart of Khmer. Lesser rubies were left in the ground or discarded as unworthy. The place is likely littered with rubies. A man with your skills could slip in and out at will and accumulate a vast fortune."

Guo's eyes narrowed. "What's to keep you from doing the same?"

"First, I don't have your skills. Second, I don't have your connections. The circle I work in doesn't buy rubies by the pound."

Guo mulled the offer. "A scorpion boat is tied up under the house. It is yours, but with all the payment up front."

"All of it? That's more than the boat is worth."

"You three are going up against Khong. I'll have to buy another boat if you don't come back."

"We're coming back," Rick said. "With my wife."

"Sure you are."

"You have a deal." Charya set the rest of the fee on Guo's desk.

Guo slid the cash across his desk, into an open drawer, and closed it. "I'll call my man to take you upriver."

"We didn't hire your man," Charya said, "just the boat."

"It's a package."

"I don't want him sneaking away and abandoning us as soon as we get to Chraknorok. I'll pilot the boat. You know I've been up and down the river many times."

Guo obviously didn't like that plan. He sighed. "Fine. Take the bigger of the two boats. Bring it back in one piece."

"I will."

Charya led the three out of the hut and back down the steps. He took his small pack from the truck and led the three down to the boat.

"This is an unwelcome start," Dara said. "That man is wrapped in bad karma."

"Karma?" Rick said.

"The cause and effect that propels life," Dara said. "Good conduct calls forth pleasant and happy results. Bad conduct opens the door to more evil outcomes. Guo is steeped in bad karma."

Rick didn't need to be convinced of that theory. He'd witnessed runs of bad luck and plenty of instances where it had seemed deserved. He turned to Charya. "You sure you can trust Guo?"

"I'm sure that I can't," Charya said. "But we need to get upriver now, and Guo's boat is our only option."

CHAPTER NINETEEN

Humphrey had no choice. His plane wasn't going anywhere without tools and that gasket material, so he had to hunt down those monkeys.

He would have preferred to do that armed, but his shotgun was on the other side of the world. As a rule, he'd found in the illicit cargo business, it was prudent to travel unarmed. Whoever he was dealing with always had more guns and men, and carrying a gun would only get him into more trouble than he could get out of.

Now he was second-guessing that rule. He hadn't considered having to fend off wildlife on one of his trips.

He might have to go out unarmed, but he wasn't going out barehanded. He searched the plane and found that the monkeys had carted off most of the easy-to-carry shiny tools. He found a hammer and tucked it into a loop of his overalls. Then he spied something better, a two-foot-long adjustable pipe wrench. He used this bulky tool to get some serious torque on the larger engine bolts. Long and hefty, he figured a swing from that would keep the little creatures at bay while he retrieved his stolen belongings. The fact that he might clobber one with what people usually referred to as a monkey wrench would just be poetic justice.

Humphrey laid the big wrench across a shoulder and exited the aircraft. He closed and locked the door behind him. He didn't trust those damn monkeys to not double back after he left and steal even more.

He adjusted his cap and set out for the spot where he'd seen the monkeys enter the jungle. The good news for Humphrey was that the creatures hadn't been stealthy. The troop of monkeys had left a clear path of broken branches and torn up ground as they had dragged their ill-gotten gains away from the plane. That was a relief because Humphrey was short on time. Eventually people would discover his plane, and the last thing he needed was to return to an empty field because some local official had dragged it off.

He soon found that while he could easily see the path the monkeys had beaten through the forest, he couldn't easily traverse it. The monkeys only broke branches under two feet tall, which left everything above that intact to smack Humphrey in the gut and face. After a half hour, the weight of the monkey wrench became a bit much, even with shifting it from shoulder to shoulder.

The humidity also took its toll. Humphrey was soon soaked in sweat all the way to his underwear. His hat drooped and slick palms threatened his grip on the wrench. It occurred to him that he'd set out on this vendetta not knowing how far he'd have to travel, and hadn't brought anything to eat or drink. He wondered if the monkeys could have high-tailed it all the way to Thailand by now.

A few minutes later, the jungle opened up to the abandoned rubber plantation Charya had talked about. Rows of spindly rubber trees stretched up a hillside. Thick, green leaves filled their crowns. Weeds and stunted bushes had popped up between all the trees.

On several, the back had been cut, and a white ooze seeped from the wound into an old tin cup strapped to the tree trunk. The plantation might have burned down and gone belly-up, but some of the less superstitious locals were still harvesting rubber sap for some extra (or primary) income.

The monkeys' trail was well-worn here, as if wherever in the jungle they came from, all roads led to the plantation. Humphrey swung the monkey wrench to a port arms kind of position and proceeded uphill.

Off to the left at the edge of the rows of trees, the ruins of a plantation house rose from a riot of encroaching jungle plants. Among charred, broken walls, chimneys still stretched for the sky. Humphrey remembered Charya telling them of the fatal fire that had consumed the plantation and taken so many lives at the same time. Despite the heat, the ominous ruins gave Humphrey a chill and he understood why the locals would assume the place was haunted.

As he continued up the row of trees along the monkeys' path, the air went still. Not just a lack of a breeze, but a lack of sound. The cacophony of insects and jungle life that had become this nightmare's soundtrack had stopped. Humphrey gripped the wrench tighter.

He could smell the monkeys before he saw them, a rank combination of musk and urine. He topped the rise in front of him and the ground leveled out on a spot without rubber trees.

In their places, there were crosses.

Scores of bamboo crosses stuck from mounds of weedy earth. These graves were haphazardly dug, irregularly spaced, and indifferently finished. Beyond the last of the bamboo crosses stood rows of formal stone tombstones. Or at least once stood. Now they were toppled and cockeyed, most of them chipped and broken.

Humphrey had seen something similar at old plantation homes around where he'd grown up. Each had a family cemetery on the property that resembled the tombstone collection at the area's far end. But the foreground crosses were something else again. He thought of the workers killed in the plantation fire, the bodies decaying in the tropical heat, far from their homes. This looked like their hasty internment near the plantation's traditional burial ground. The resilient bamboo crosses were doing their best to keep the dead from being forgotten.

From behind the furthest stone tombstone peeked the monkey that had stolen Humphrey's hat. It climbed up to the top of the canted marker and stared across the graves at Humphrey. Humphrey froze.

The monkey stood on its hind legs and screeched.

The entire troop of monkeys appeared from behind the grave markers. Each brandished something Humphrey recognized. Three carried a wrench, a screwdriver, and a breaker bar from his aircraft tools. Other monkeys held knives, a steering wheel, what looked like the shattered legs of chairs. It seemed his tools hadn't been the monkeys' only plunder.

The monkeys began a slow advance, not a threatening charge to bluff for dominance, but a measured roll forward like a tide destined to submerge all before it. They picked their way through the makeshift graveyard, crisscrossing paths until each monkey climbed up and settled on a specific bamboo marker. There they paused and eyed Humphrey like ravenous men before a plate of steaks.

Humphrey stepped back and heard a crunch beneath his feet. He looked down to see he'd crushed a bleached human skull. That startled him and he hopped back. He'd been so focused on looking ahead he hadn't been looking down. He stood on an entire skeleton. And the bones were not alone. To the right and left lay several other skeletons, all at different stages of bleaching and decay.

What was it Charya said? Humphrey thought. *Yeah, vengeful spirits haunted this place.*

These monkeys looked a heck of a lot like vengeful spirits to Humphrey, and he bet the poor guys rotting away under his feet had thought the same thing. He imagined the monkeys toppling the gravestones of the plantation owners, then baiting more victims in by stealing their things.

While his initial plan had been to return to the plane with his gasket material and tools, now it was to return with his life.

The lead monkey screeched a war cry. The rest of the troop leapt from their crosses and charged Humphrey.

CHAPTER TWENTY

Humphrey sprinted away from the graveyard.

Sprinting surprised him almost as much as the monkey attack. He hadn't sprinted since a German Fokker chased him off an aerodrome in Northern France during the war. But while his brain told him he could sprint, his muscles soon corrected him and told him he most definitely could not. Stabbing pain raced from his calves to his thighs and threatened to stop him in his tracks.

From behind came the cries of more monkeys than he wanted to count, and from a much closer distance than he wanted to admit. Despite the pain, he pumped his legs harder.

He'd seen these monkeys run after they pillaged his plane. Even if he'd still been eighteen years old, he wouldn't be able to outrun them. This situation was not going to end well.

A knife sailed past him, so close to his ear that he heard a whoosh of air. It embedded itself in a rubber tree ahead of him. Then a bottle struck him in the shoulder. Monkeys didn't have those kinds of throwing skills. If Humphrey thought he needed some kind of sign that these creatures had a paranormal connection to the dead plantation workers, he had it now.

One monkey charged ahead of the others. It leapt off the ground and onto Humphrey's leg. Sharp claws dug into his flesh. Humphrey screamed.

He sent the monkey wrench on a quick downward swing. Its head caught the clinging monkey at its shoulder. The monkey squealed and went tumbling backward onto the ground.

"Score one for me," Humphrey said.

But the others didn't learn from the first monkey's mistake. Two, then three ran alongside Humphrey. They dodged tree trunks and waited for a clear path to leap at him.

Humphrey reached the edge of the rubber tree stand. The ground sloped down a dozen yards to thicker growth. Humphrey tried to stop but momentum would not be denied. He hit the edge, his feet slipped out from under him, and down he went. His butt hit the ground and he continued on a rapid, downward slide. He dropped the monkey wrench and grabbed his hat with both hands.

From the dark recesses of the plants below, two yellow eyes blinked open. Humphrey was sliding right for them. Humphrey's heart jumped into his throat.

A tiger's roar ripped through the air. A huge orange and black head burst from the bushes. Humphrey had never seen a tiger this big, and never so close without a set of bars between them. The big cat's muscles rippled as it bounded up the slope at Humphrey.

This is going to be one awful way to die, Humphrey thought.

The cat pounced. It launched itself uphill with a twin thrust from its rear legs. But instead of landing on Humphrey, it arced over him. Its trailing foot creased Humphrey's hat and he clamped it tighter to his head. The tiger landed uphill.

Humphrey rolled sideways and came to a stop on his chest.

Uphill, the tiger attacked the monkeys. They scrambled about for an escape, but the tiger had too many targets within its reach to miss them all. Monkeys wailed as feline claws slashed simian fur and shattered bones.

Maybe the tiger had been aiming for him and missed. Maybe the tiger had a running feud with the pack of possessed monkeys. Maybe the big cat was just as ornery as the monkeys were and was spoiling for a fight with anything. Humphrey didn't care one whit about the why of his situation. All he cared about was that it gave him a chance to escape.

The tiger and the monkeys became a snarling blur of black, orange, and brown. Blood splattered the trees and ground around the whirling melee. Humphrey pushed himself off the ground and skirted the edge of the plantation at a lumbering run until he found the spot where he'd arrived.

He leaned against a tree and pressed down on his cap. It felt wrong.

He took it off and checked it. A tear ran through the middle. That tiger's claw had damn near parted Humphrey's hair in a permanent way. Bad enough it had ruined his new hat. He sighed.

A quick search of the ground revealed the monkeys' trail that would lead him back to his plane.

But he was going back without the gasket material, and without any of the tools the monkeys had stolen. And now he'd just voluntarily added his big monkey wrench to their collection. He was officially worse off than before he left the plane to come here. He was literally going back empty-handed.

Then he saw the tree where someone had been tapping rubber sap. An idea came to him. A desperate, risky idea, for sure, but compared to having no ideas, it seemed pretty good.

He wouldn't be returning to the plane empty handed after all.

CHAPTER TWENTY-ONE

Charya, Rick, and Dara stopped at the muddy Mekong's shore. Tied off there were two weathered, wooden boats that looked like they had been around since before the French even knew about Cambodia. The larger of them was about sixteen feet long and five feet wide with an upturned, pointed bow and stern. The boat rode low enough in the water that climbing in would be no problem.

Rick couldn't say the same for staying afloat with the weight of the three of them aboard.

Charya untied the bowline and took up a position at the bow. "Help Dara in and then we'll push off."

Rick gave Dara a hand doing an awkward one-armed roll into the boat. Then he and Charya pushed it away from the shore and climbed in. The boat began a slow, downriver float. Once inside, Rick noticed two disconcerting things: a missing deck plank revealed a fetid inch of standing water along the keel, and a long pole beside his seat. He remembered seeing similar boats down at Phnom Penh and the men in them were poling the boats around the docks.

Rick picked up the pole. "This pole is going to get us up upriver faster than Khong's men can drive?"

"No." Charya opened a panel in the stern. "This is."

Under the panel was an inboard engine that looked like it had been salvaged from a motorcycle. Charya set a few switches and then reached in and pulled a starter cord. The engine sputtered to life. Charya dropped the hatch and muffled the engine racket. He took a seat at the tiller, pointed the boat upstream, and then eased a tiny throttle lever forward. The engine spooled up and the little boat began to knife through the water.

Rick slid over to Charya and took out the map. "So how long will this trip take?"

Charya looked over the map and pointed to a spot on the river. "We're here, so most of the day, maybe all of it depending on the current. You and I will take turns steering and sleeping."

"As will I," Dara said. "It only takes one arm to steer."

"Indeed it does," Charya said.

Charya's pack contained food and water he'd stopped and purchased during their trip to Guo's shack. Rick was glad that Charya had thought ahead about that, because Rick sure hadn't and Charya's plan looked like a two-day trip.

Over the next hour or so, they passed several similar boats heading downstream as well as a few struggling upstream without the help of an inboard motor. All carried peasant Cambodians and light cargoes and a few live animals. The Mekong was doing here what highways did back home in Georgia, but at one hell of a slower pace.

Soon Charya had to admit he was struggling to stay awake. Dara took a turn at the tiller and Charya stretched out in the bow and went to sleep. Rick took a seat beside the old man. As the sun dipped lower in the sky, he decided now was a good time to get some questions answered.

"Charya said that the followers of Rudra were defeated by King Jayavarman VII in a surprise attack."

"A true story," Dara said, "that still omits half the truth. Since we had been entrusted with the Scarlet Heart, the king's emissary told our abbot rest of the story, one so awful, the abbot was sworn to never let the details of it leave the monastery."

"But you are going to tell me?"

"Only because the monastery has been destroyed, the Scarlet Heart taken, and these are details you will need to know."

Rick didn't like the sound of any of that.

"Rudra's followers wanted to add insult to injury," Dara said, "to have the king feel his defeat to the depths of his soul. It wasn't just any woman they forced to become Rudra's vessel. They had raided the king's summer palace, and kidnapped the queen. They wanted the king to face Rudra in the guise of his wife, to gaze upon pure evil radiated from her eyes, hear foul curses uttered from her lips, and experience death at her lovely hands."

"That's horrible."

"When the king confronted Rudra resurrected, the rebels' plan worked. You can imagine the impact on the king, how he could be forgiven a moment's hesitation confronted by a wife possessed. The horror and disbelief would be overwhelming. And for the king, it almost was."

"But he prevailed."

"And she did not. The king and queen's marriage had been more political than romantic. The emotional bond between them was not strong enough to keep the king from doing his duty. He drove Rudra back to her prison on another plane. Rudra exacted revenge by killing her unwilling host before leaving."

"Why are you telling me all these details?" Rick said. "The end of the story is the same."

"Because I know life is all cycles: birth, death, and rebirth. How we lived our past guides our future."

Rick had more of a "one-and-done" attitude about life, but he let the abbot continue.

"We are stepping into a repeating event. Men are about to try crossing Rudra over into our realm again. When history plays out this time, Rose will have the role of the victim queen. We will have the role played by the king. Karma favors our victory, but does not guarantee it."

"I'm not worried. I've gambled big and won before. I'm ready." Rick had also gambled big and lost, but this wasn't the time to dwell on that.

"I'm not sure you are ready, any more ready than King Jayavarman was. No one can be prepared to see a loved one possessed and transformed by a demonic god. And if karma helps us complete this circle as the last one was, your wife will be a casualty. I don't think anyone can be prepared for that, either."

The idea of life without Rose wasn't anything Rick wanted to consider. 'We'll all make it through this. I can do it."

"Rudra believes otherwise, or she would not have selected Rose."

"Rudra underestimated our marriage bond."

"That strength will be your weakness. The king could fight the image of a woman he did not love. Can you fight the image of one you do?"

"We'll be there before Khong has a chance to do a thing to Rose. And even if he does, whatever Rudra's done to her, Rosie will be in there somewhere. She'll come through. We always have for each other."

"You have supported each other in the sun and rain," Dara said. "You are about to be hit by a monsoon."

A few hours later, Charya awakened, surprisingly refreshed for a man who slept in such an uncomfortable position. He encouraged Rick to grab some sleep as the sun dipped below the trees.

"I'm feeling pretty good," Rick said.

"Take this chance while it is here and everything is calm. The Mekong is never as peaceful as it seems. I have travelled up it many times, and the only thing that is predictable, is that what is around the next bend never is."

CHAPTER TWENTY-TWO

Hours later, Rick awakened to uncounted stiff muscles and a sunrise that felt like sand in his eyes.

The best sleeping position he'd been able to manage was with his back on the deck, his head elevated on one seat and his knees on another. Add in the slap of water against the hull, the dead fish stink coming up from the bilge, and the grumble of the motor, and he counted himself lucky to have gotten the intermittent sleep that he had. He sat up and gave his back and shoulders a painful stretch.

Dara lay curled up in the bow. The diminutive monk could fit in a space Rick couldn't. The abbot also had his spine curled to a degree Rick would have been certain was physically impossible. Meditation exercises had given Dara and his monks some impressive control over their bodies and pain.

Charya sat at the tiller, piloting the boat up the placid river. "Have a good sleep?"

"Like a night at the Waldorf Astoria. How are you managing?"

"Sunrise seems to have given me a second wind. I can finish out my turn at the tiller."

Rick's attention turned to food and water. He found a water bottle and took a swig. In the normal world he'd be heading straight for a morning shower. Days in the jungle and a night in a filthy fishing boat had resulted in a level of dirty that he hadn't thought was possible.

He looked over the side at the muddy Mekong and decided that a scrub with that water would not only make him dirtier, there was a good chance it would make him sick.

He sat back up and noticed a man on the western shore, half-obscured by vegetation. He wore a loose-fitting black shirt and sported a conical thatch hat festooned with a camouflage of palm leaves and other vegetation. He stared at the boat as it approached.

"Do you see that guy over there?" Rick asked Charya.

Charya looked in the man's direction. A grim look crossed his face and he steered the boat for the center of the river. The man in the thatched hat retreated into the foliage. Then a strange kind of bird call sounded from that location.

"Bad news," Charya said. "From the way he was dressed, that man was one of the Lao bandits who prey along this stretch of the river. He just signaled others in his band that we are coming upriver."

"Who are the Lao?"

"The people from further up the Mekong. They claimed some of this area, but the French declared it Cambodian. They started out rebelling against the French, but turned to banditry as a more profitable enterprise."

"We don't have anything onboard worth stealing."

"They won't know that until after they've killed us."

A rifle fired from the western riverbank. A bullet struck the gunwale a foot away from Rick and delivered chips of wood into his lap. He dove for the deck.

Charya hunched over and pushed the throttle to wide open. The scream of the engine was out of proportion to the minor increase in speed.

Apparently seeing no one returning fire, the bandits became emboldened. Several stepped out from the trees, all wearing what looked like black pajamas to Rick. They raised rifles to their shoulders, aimed, and fired. Bullets whizzed by just over the transom.

Dara's head poked up from the bow. "What's going on?"

"Stay down, Dara," Charya said. "We've met up with bandits."

Dara ducked back down like a turtle retreating into its shell.

More gunfire came from the shore. The men were finding the boat's range and several bullets hit the hull. One struck a weak part in the wood and blasted open a hole a few inches wide.

"Pull up that hatch in the deck," Charya said.

Rick crawled over to a long, narrow hatch cover. He yanked at its handle and the hatch came free. Rick cast it aside. In the hold were two older model bolt-action rifles. Not impressive, but two of a kind beat having no cards at all as far as Rick was concerned. "Woo hoo!"

"That was what Guo meant when he said we got the scorpion boat," Charya said. "It comes with a pair of claws. With those we'll ambush the truck carrying Rose."

"Looks like we get to do some practice with them first." Rick plucked one of the rifles from the hiding place. He pulled at the bolt to check if it was loaded.

The bolt didn't move.

He feared rust had done a number on this gun as it sat in the damp hold. He was going to have to break the bolt free. Then he took a closer look at it. The bolt wasn't rusted in place. It was welded. He glanced at the other rifle and it was welded as well.

More bullets slammed into the hull and splashed in the water by the boat.

Rick showed the gun's breech to Charya. "Your pal Guo has screwed us over."

"More than you know," Charya said. "He's well connected with these bandits. It's a big coincidence they were laying here in wait for us when it is clear we have nothing to steal."

From downstream came the roar of a boat motor. A late model skiff with a pair of large outboard motors headed their way. The nose rode high and a V of frothy wakes trailed behind the craft. Rick didn't need to see men in black pajamas onboard to know Lao bandits piloted it.

"We're not outrunning that boat," Rick said.

Charya shot a quick glance over his shoulder. "You're right. We'll need to beach the boat and hope we lose them in the jungle."

Charya aimed the boat toward the eastern shore. That was the opposite side of the river from Chraknorok and Rose. Rick wondered how they were going to get back across without a boat.

One look back at the approaching skiff and he realized that was a moot point. The bandits were going to intercept them before they even got close enough to jump out and wade ashore.

Charya figured out the same thing. He picked the rifle up from the deck. "Grab that other gun from the hold. We'll use them as clubs and go out fighting. Dara, you keep your head down up there so it doesn't get shot off."

More rounds came from the western bank. One smacked into the bow near Dara's head. Another struck the engine with a thunk. The motor coughed and died. The sharp smell of gasoline filled the air.

Rick knew their fate was sealed, and with it, Rose's. He stood with the rifle in his hand like a baseball bat, literally ready to go down swinging.

The gunfire from the shore stopped as the bandits' boat roared up beside them and then crossed their bow. Three black-clad men stood in the skiff ahead of the pilot. Two had rifles. One held a Thompson submachine gun. Rick's rifle-turned-club wasn't going to do much good.

The boat made a full circle around them. The heavy wake battered them from all sides and brought the boat to a halt. The bandits' boat stopped off their bow.

The man with the Tommy gun shouted some orders in a language Rick didn't understand. He fully understood the tone, the body language, and the gun barrel pointed at him. They were going to surrender or they were going to die.

Dara rose up from where he'd been hiding in the bow. He faced the bandits with his back straight and left hand on his hip.

The demeanor of the bandits changed, like someone had dumped the air out of their sails.

Then Dara laid into them with a powerful barrage of sentences in the same dialect they'd used. Two of the men exchanged some confused sounding replies. With every statement Dara made, the bandits looked a little more cowed.

Then the man piloting the boat throttled up the engines and headed back downriver. He shouted orders to the men on the riverbank and they retreated into the jungle.

Rick dropped down into the seat and exhaled in relief. "What just happened?"

Dara grinned. "I told them you two were taking me on a sacred pilgrimage to the headwaters of the Mekong. I asked them if they were ready to endure the bad karma of hurting an abbot or even delaying his journey."

"Dara's presence took them by surprise," Charya said. "One said to the other that Guo didn't say there was an abbot on board, that this had to be the wrong boat."

"Those men may have been bandits," Dara said, "but they were still Buddhists and respected the clergy."

"You know there was a good chance they wouldn't," Rick said.

"I was certain we were not destined to die here on the river."

Rick didn't want to ask if that was because Dara knew they were destined to die elsewhere.

Charya turned and inspected the engine. He stuck his finger in a big hole in its side. "This isn't going to be starting anytime soon."

Their boat had already drifted downstream, the exact wrong direction to save Rose.

Charya pulled out two oars hidden under the seats and handed one to Rick. "Now we row. It isn't much farther."

Rick took the oar. Even if it wasn't much farther, they were going to get there far slower. And every minute lost meant it was more likely Rose would already be hidden away in Chraknorok by the time they got there.

CHAPTER TWENTY-THREE

Despite the blindfold, Rose was certain they'd arrived at Chraknorok even before the truck stopped moving.

Suddenly, she felt a sense of dread, the same feeling she got watching a line of storm clouds approach from the horizon. This dread was followed by a new level of fear that landed like a bowling ball to the gut. And it hit in an instant.

Moments later the truck began to bounce and buck more, and Rose imagined that they'd transitioned from the packed earth road to some kind of paved one, probably made of flat stone blocks, and from the uneven nature of them, probably made a long time ago.

Then Rose sensed a presence. It felt like a gust of hot, fetid air that hit her in the face and then enveloped her body. Terror welled up inside her, the kind of subconscious, natural revulsion and fear one gets when seeing a snake or other inherently dangerous animal that triggers an inborn threat to self-preservation. But this danger was greater than any natural predator could inspire. This malevolent force seemed to threaten Rose's soul.

The truck lurched to a stop. Tiang whipped off Rose's blindfold. The light hurt her eyes for a moment while they adjusted. He dragged her out of the vehicle.

Khong had indeed found Chraknorok. They stood before the ruins of a temple, and not the kind of overgrown, under-maintained edifices Rose had seen in newspapers and magazines. This temple had been leveled, reduced to a pile of large, broken blocks. Charya's story about the king's army destroying Chraknorok had been true. Only the toppled tower before her gave any indication of what the rubble had once been. And seeing that tower made her break out in a cold sweat.

Carved into the block near the peak was the figure of a woman with four arms. Patches of peeling blue paint hinted at the color she had once been finished in. In her lower sets of arms she carried a bow and a sword. Her upper arms stretched out forward, palms up. That was the same stance she'd seen Tiang in when he'd used some kind of supernatural force to attack the monastery.

The carving had to be of Rudra. As Rose looked at it, the suffocating cloud of evil about her seemed to contract and it became hard to breathe.

A raspy woman's voice sounded in her head. "Mine!"

Rose's knees locked and she could not break free of the carving's gaze. Only Tiang yanking her by the arm broke the spell. As she stumbled along beside him, she remembered the question he'd asked her.

Do you think you can stand tall against the power of a god?

Now she wasn't sure she could.

Just ahead of her lay two piles of block and stone. They bracketed a set of steps that descended into the earth. A line of men and women exited the stairs, straining as they carried huge chunks of rock. The line snaked to a third pile a hundred feet away, where the unfortunates dropped their stones, and then trudged back to the underground stairway.

The poor souls hauling the stones wore ragged clothing, a few little more than loincloths. Sandals fashioned from tires or bamboo shod their feet. They were all small, and by the general looks of them Rose guessed indigenous. By the demeanor of them, she was certain they labored involuntarily.

Then she saw proof of their enslavement. One of Khong's ex-pat thugs patrolled the line with a rifle at the ready and a machete at his belt. Every now and then he smacked a laborer with the rifle butt. The grin on the guard's face said the unwarranted abuse was for the guard's pleasure.

Tiang led Rose and the men from the truck to the entrance. The guard paused the laborers' progression from Hell so Tiang's group could descend the stairs. Rose caught the eyes of a few of the laborers. Each time they reacted with even greater fear at seeing her arrival, as if she was the last piece to be added to the awful machine they had been building. Rudra's legend was certainly no secret among them.

Tiang and Rose descended the steps while the rest of the men went elsewhere, and seemed relieved to do so. That didn't make Rose feel any better about what awaited her below.

The stone steps were centuries old, worn in the center from millions of footfalls. The passage was barely wide enough for two people abreast, and the once-smooth walls showed pockmarks and stress cracks. This damage wasn't caused by soldiers toppling stone walls. The force the king had used to level Chraknorok had shaken even this mighty temple to its foundation. At a time in history without modern explosives, only something supernatural could have done that.

During her and Rick's adventures, Rose had been in several underground chambers over the years. In every instance, the subterranean passages were always cooler than the surface temperature. To her surprise, that wasn't true here. As they descended the steps, the air grew warmer and more humid. Twenty feet down, the stairway ended at a short hallway. Oil lamps burned in holders along the walls. Tiang gave Rose a shove to keep her moving.

The hallway ended at a T-intersection. Tiang pushed Rose to the left. What lay ahead looked like more of a maze than a set of passageways. She passed by rooms that were either empty or partially collapsed as well as doorways completely blocked by rubble. The unfortunates she'd seen outside had been clearing this complex for a while, and still had a long way to go. Even if she could get away, she'd never find her way out of here.

Worse yet, when Rick came to the rescue, he would never find his way in.

One of the thugs came around a corner and blocked their way.

"Khong wants you," he said. "Ain't a bit happy you got so many men killed."

Tiang's face went red. "The fat man has become too lazy to do the hard work, but not to question the outcome."

The two were paying no attention to Rose. She stepped back against the wall and slid the rosewood disc from her pocket. Without looking, she pressed hard and drew a symbol on the stone wall. She felt the hardwood grind against the stone. She hoped that it ground away enough to leave a mark.

The thug grinned at Tiang's anger.

Tiang raised a hand, palm-first at the man. "You seem to have forgotten to be respectful."

The thug's jaw dropped. "Now there, I'm just the messenger." He backed away. "Take it up with the boss. He's in the Chamber of Rebirth."

Tiang practically growled as he grabbed Rose by the shoulder and shoved her forward past the thug.

Every now and then one of the stone-laden slaves would appear in the tunnel and be filled with terror at the sight of Tiang. He would drop the rock and flatten himself against the wall to give Rose and Tiang room to pass. Rose still had to turn sideways each time, which gave her a closeup view of the workers' faces. Sunken, frightened eyes gazed out from over sallow cheeks.

Many had recent bruising. All had scars. She had a whole new reason to hate Khong, Tiang, and their cadre of sordid mercenaries.

At each turn, Tiang guided Rose with a push, shove, or pull. Each time she exaggerated the impact and grazed the closest wall. That just made Tiang angrier. It was a risk she knew she had to take.

The passage they were in became twice as wide and the ceiling moved several feet higher. More oil lamps dimly lit the area. Makeshift log columns supported the cracked and canted ceiling. Chunks of the ceiling lay on a floor finished in broken and chipped ceramic tiles. Other bits from the stone walls lay near the walls, where exhausted slave laborers leaned against the stone.

The walls contained the remains of more murals dedicated to Rudra. There was a scene of her vanquishing armies as power radiated from her hands, a scene of her beheading a dozen with one slash of her sword, another with her standing amidst a ruined temple with the bodies of slain Buddhist monks beneath her feet. Rose had read about murals like these. The pictures were supposed to spur the audience to contemplate the power they were about to kneel before. She'd never known such art to be so completely dedicated to violence and bloodshed.

At the sight of Tiang, the slave laborers jumped to their feet. Men stooped, hoisted heavy rocks, and headed for the hallway. Other men laden with stone approached from a doorway at the far end of the room. Tiang pushed Rose in the direction of that doorway.

As they passed one of the log supports, the timber moaned and ground stone snowed from the crack in the ceiling above it.

"This place looks like it could collapse at any moment," Rose said.

"These repairs only need to be temporary," Tiang said. "Once Rudra is released, the temple ruins will be left behind, and the world will be conquered."

As soon as they entered the next room, Rose felt that terrifying sense of dread roll back in with a vengeance. The room reminded Rose of a Roman amphitheater, shaped like a slice of pie with the pointed end in front of her. Rings of stone benches stretched out on both sides and down thirty feet to a stage in front. More debris littered the area and laborers picked through it looking for pieces they could carry. In several spots, men with sledgehammers smashed larger rocks into smaller ones.

Tiang led Rose down a set of central steps to the stage. In the center of the stage, against the rear wall, stood a statue of Rudra surrounded by bamboo scaffolding. Two sweating men in loincloths were working on the figure.

The face was unmistakably Rudra's, with the same malicious expression. The legs were set right foot forward, knees flexed, much more of a hunter's stance than the usual shoulder-width-apart pose most statues used. Her upper arms were raised over her head, with a sword in each hand. The rust-coated blades made Rose think they were actual metal. Rudra's two lower arms were stretched out in front of her. The left already had a jade hand affixed. One of the two men was bent over the right fitting the other jade hand. The other man was painting the statue in an iridescent blue. It sparked in the light of the oil lamps like something reflective was embedded in the paint.

A wave of nausea rocked Rose. She teetered and had to touch one of the benches to keep from falling over. That presence she thought she had felt before was centered here in this room, and she was certain it resided in that statue. It was calling Rose forward. No, not calling. A call could be ignored. Rudra was drawing Rose forward, like a rod reeling in a hooked fish.

Tiang stopped them halfway down the steps. An enormous Cambodian man sat in a wide, cushioned chair. Some benches had been torn away and the chair set in their space. Sweat speckled the man's face and bald head. Rose figured this had to be Khong. He fanned himself with a palm leaf fan. The gang leader paused when he saw Tiang.

"The guards said you'd arrived," Khong said. "You have the Scarlet Heart?"

Tiang reached into his pocket and took out a wad of cloth. He unfolded it to reveal the largest ruby, even the largest jewel of any kind that Rose had ever seen. The four-inch-long, marquis-cut gem practically glowed, as if it absorbed the light around it, and then amplified and returned it. The effect was simultaneously awe-inspiring and terrifying.

Khong's eyes went wide at the sight. His lips curled into the kind of revolting smile addicts displayed before taking their drug of choice. He reached for the jewel. Tiang moved it away.

"I would not do that," he said. "The Scarlet Heart of Khmer prefers to not be handled, especially by those unprepared or unworthy."

Khong's eyes narrowed at being labeled as unworthy. He made a grab for the rock.

A wavy pulse like she'd seen Tiang create blasted from the jewel and struck Khong's hand. He cried out and pulled it back like he'd been electrocuted.

"Don't be ashamed," Tiang said. "Rudra repelled even the pious monks who guarded it."

Khong didn't look ashamed. He looked furious.

Tiang held the ruby nearer his face. The reddish glow gave him a Satanic look. "Rudra commands unlimited power. Rest assured that she will be magnanimous sharing it with those who released her."

The anger in Khong's eyes said that he wasn't used to having anyone, even the high priest of a powerful god, tell him what to do. Rather than lash out at Tiang, he turned to Rose. "What is she doing here?"

"Behold, Rudra's vessel. The next time you see this woman, she will be a god."

"Not if I can help it," Rose said.

"And of course, you can't," Tiang said.

"You said you needed to prepare the vessel to accept Rudra," Khong said. "You did that?"

"She is prepared. That saves us from kidnapping a woman from the area, and her exotic features will please Rudra."

Normally Rose would have been happy to be referred to as exotic, but not in this context.

"When will we be ready for the ritual?" Khong said.

Tiang appraised the work done on the statue. "These men's work should be done soon. Then I will need to purify the statue. Then we can begin."

"Until then," Khong said, "lock her up and have her watched. The last thing we need is for something to happen to the vessel."

"I'm not a vessel," Rose said. "I have a name."

"Which will soon change to Rudra," Khong said. "Get her out of here."

Tiang returned the Scarlet Heart to his pocket, grabbed Rose's elbow, and began to drag her back up the steps. She jerked her elbow from his grip. Tiang pushed her forward and she ascended the steps with as much dignity as she could muster.

They passed through the anteroom and Tiang ordered one of the armed goons there to follow them. They entered the hallway again. This time they turned off to the left. Tiang stopped them in front of a room that had been only half cleared of debris. He shoved Rose into it.

"Make sure she stays here," he said to the thug. "And make sure she isn't harmed."

The thug nodded. Tiang walked away and the man leaned back against the wall opposite the doorway. He lit a cigarette and stared at Rose.

Small as it was, the oil lamps in the hall still barely lit the room. Rose took a seat on one of the toppled blocks and sighed.

An almost endless list of problems painted Rose a grim picture: a guard outside the room, any number of goons between the doorway and the exit, zero chance that a fair-skinned redhead would pass through the temple ruins unnoticed. Even if she did, then there were miles of jungle between Chraknorok and anyone who might care enough to help her, if she could find someone who would. She couldn't see a way to get out of here.

She had to hope that Rick could find a way in.

***

Tiang returned to the Chamber of Rebirth. The leaders of Chraknorok had built this temple and this underground amphitheater beneath it for one purpose, to bring Rudra into our realm. He imagined how it must have been centuries ago with the room lit by hundreds of lamps, every surface polished and new, and the seats filled with Rudra's passionate devoted. These people had suffered under the king's oppression, then worked hard to build this city and overthrow him. The anticipation over Rudra's liberation had to have been intense.

Yet no more than his own.

From the moment he'd set foot in the Phenum Aoral temple as an initiate, he'd sensed the power of the Scarlet Heart of Khmer. That amazed him, but the truly shocking part of it was that none of the other initiates could. As the years went on, he discovered the monks there could not either. They all believed it was within the vault, but they did not *feel* its presence. Connecting with the jewel was a gift that only he possessed.

Soon the gift began to give more.

Rudra herself began to speak to him. He heard her voice, her commands, as clear as if she had been standing beside him. She offered him any part of the world he wished, if he would set her free. His studies at the monastery had taught him in detail how the leaders of Chraknorok had done it, so the ritual was no problem. However, finding the statue and its missing parts *was* a problem. It would take resources he would never have. So his first stop after abandoning the monastery was Khong.

Tiang wasn't surprised at all that a power-hungry sociopath with no moral code instantly embraced the idea of bringing Rudra back to our reality. Tiang's small lie that Rudra had specifically asked for Khong's help had sealed the deal. Tiang passed on the location of Chraknorok that Rudra had given him, and Khong sent his expedition to that spot first thing. The city's discovery cemented Tiang's position in Khong's hierarchy.

He only needed to remain in Khong's good graces for a little while longer. Then the gangster's role as useful idiot would no longer be necessary.

And now Tiang was about to make that time period even shorter by completing the reassembly of Rudra's statue.

Khong had left the hall. He preferred his above ground quarters and that suited Tiang just fine. Only the two men on the scaffold remained in the hall. Tiang descended past the seats and to the base of the scaffolding. The two men paused their work and gave Tiang a fearful look. Everyone at Chraknorok had seen him wield the power Rudra had entrusted to him. None wanted to be on the receiving end of it.

"Both of you," Tiang said, "out until I call you back."

The two did not waste time replying. They scrambled to the other side of the scaffolding and climbed down fast enough to make monkeys proud. Then they sprinted up the steps between the seats and out into the anteroom.

Chraknorok had been built over a location where the overlap between the two realities was weak, all the better to make Rudra's return easier. This close to that thin spot, Tiang could draw even more of Rudra's power.

He lowered his arms to his side and faced his palms downward. He spoke the magic incantation in his mind. The air beneath his hands began to compress and expand in alternating waves. At its most powerful, this gift had leveled the Phenum Aoral monastery. At this lower amplitude and frequency, it levitated Tiang.

He rose up the side of the scaffold until he was even with the head. A twist of his wrists nudged him over the scaffolding. He closed his fists and set down before Rudra's eyes. This close, their huge size was intimidating, or at least would have been to lesser men.

Tiang took the cloth wrapping the Scarlet Heart of Khmer from his pocket. He rolled the jewel out into his palm and cast the cloth aside. It fluttered down to the ground like a dying bird.

Tiang raised the ruby and aligned it with the recess between the statue's eyes. If the return of the hands was any indicator, he wouldn't even have to set the jewel in place.

And he did not have to. As if propelled by a vacuum, the jewel flew from his fingertips and embedded itself in the recess on the forehead. The jade hands had done the exact same thing once they were inches from the arms. What the king had torn asunder, Rudra wanted made whole again.

The ruby flared to life as if it had been plugged into a socket. A dazzling red aura bathed Tiang. Then the statue's eyes took on a similar red glow. That shocked Tiang because the eyes were the same solid stone as the rest of the statue. He took a half step back. Beneath him, the jade hands pulsed a vibrant green.

The scaffolding shuddered as power surged through the statue. The stone expanded and then returned to normal, like an athlete flexing its muscles. Then the eyes dimmed back to gray stone, the jade hands' light faded, and finally the Scarlet Heart went dark.

Rudra had rewarded his faithful servant with a demonstration of her power. Tiang felt blessed.

Tiang's heart soared. Everything was about to transpire just as prophesized. He would call the workers back in to finish their restoration, then he would perform the sanctification ritual. Once all that was completed, the vessel would be offered during the rebirth ceremony. Rudra would return, and the two of them would remake the world in her image.

CHAPTER TWENTY-FOUR

Rick raised his head above the top of a riot of ferns and put Charya's binoculars to his eyes. Charya and Dara had already looked over the ruins and now he was taking a turn at it.

The map in the gangsters' truck had been dead on. The remains of Chraknorok lay about fifty yards away. And remains was the best way to describe it. After King Jayavarman's ravage and a few hundred years of tropical weather, the place looked more like an oversized jumble of children's blocks than a Cambodian city.

The first distressing sight was the parade of laborers trooping in and out of an excavated underground entrance. They carried out heavy chunks of stone they then discarded in a pile. Dressed in rags and stooped from hard work, there wasn't a chance in Hell these men weren't slaves. The two rifle-toting thugs watching the procession of the damned confirmed that status.

The second, and much more distressing, sight was the truck parked near one of the ruins. Rick would bet the deed to their shop that it was the same truck that had been at the monastery. That meant that their delay along the river had cost them dearly. Rose was already here. If the lack of working firearms hadn't been enough to doom the intercept and rescue plan, it was doomed now.

Rick sat down and sighed. He handed the binoculars back to Charya. "Looks like we bet big and lost."

"Not yet," Charya said.

"We don't even know where the Rudra statue is in that big pile of rocks," Rick said, "if it is even there at all."

"It is there," Dara said. "That pile there over the underground entrance is what is left of the temple to

Rudra and Chamber of Rebirth. Even from here I can see the inscriptions to Rudra on the toppled tower. And the Scarlet Heart lies beneath those ruins."

"You mean you guess it does," Rick said.

"I know it does. I've spent almost all my life in proximity to the Scarlet Heart. Only the Companions have spent more time with it. It radiates a sensation of impending danger, like a tiger confined in a cage. That sensation is coming from beneath the temple."

"I don't feel anything."

"Few do. One must have the disposition to be attuned to such things. I was selected as the abbot because I do."

"And Tiang also had that disposition?" Charya said.

"Indeed."

"And so he wasn't just a monk who'd abandoned the monastery," Charya said. "He was your chosen successor because he shared your gift."

"No one stays in one life forever. It is foolish to plan as if one would. But while Tiang had my gift, he did not have my strength of will to ignore Rudra's temptations. My mistake in selecting him as an initiate has led to where we are now. So you will understand why I am so committed to being part of setting things right."

Hope swelled inside Rick. "If you're sure the Scarlet Heart is there, then Rose would be there, too. I mean, they need her for the ceremony, so why hold her far away, right?"

"I would agree," Dara said.

"Then we need to go in and get her out," Rick said.

"And retrieve the Scarlet Heart," Dara said. "As well as the jade hands. We must reset all the safeguards King Jayavarman put in place."

"I don't think the men with the rifles will let us walk in and out," Charya said.

"I don't know," Rick said, "they're letting all those workers walk in and out."

"We're too tall and too completely dressed to pass as one of those poor slaves."

Rick took back the binoculars and scanned the ruins again, as well as where the truck was parked at the edge of the city. "I can see the two guards watching the slaves, but there's no one else near the ruins. The only other goon is down by the truck where the road ends at the ruin's edge."

"They are more worried about the slaves escaping," Charya said, "than repelling intruders from the outside."

"It's a lost city in the middle of a jungle," Rick said. "Khong killed any potentially disloyal people who knew the location. It figures that he wouldn't be worried about unwelcome visitors."

"The laborers will stop working when it gets dark," Dara said. "The guards wouldn't want to be out here when tigers start to prowl."

Neither did Rick. "I hadn't even considered adding tigers to my list of problems. Thanks for that."

"Once night falls," Charya said, "we could slip in that entrance unobserved."

"That's a long time from now," Rick said. "Who knows what could happen to Rose while I'm sitting out here doing nothing."

"And Tiang and Khong have everything they need to start the ritual," Dara said. "It could begin at any time, though I don't sense that it has started yet."

"Then we need a distraction," Charya said, "so you two can sneak in past the guards."

"Just us two?" Rick said. "What about you?"

"I'm the distraction. You two circle around to that jumble of rocks on the right. I'll wander over there, halfway between the truck and the entrance. That will draw the guards over. Then you two sneak in. I'm guessing those poor slaves won't rat you out. Anyone who might set them free should be welcome."

Rick thought the plan had a lot of risk to it. The guards might see them. There could be guards just inside the entrance. This entrance might not even be the one that led to the Chamber of Rebirth or where Rose was being held.

But if Rose was the stakes at this table, he'd play any hand he was dealt.

"I'm in," he said.

Minutes later, he and Dara knelt secreted behind what remained of a building wall. From here, their line of sight included the guards, the slaves adding to the rock pile, and the truck beyond. They were close enough to the entrance and the line of laborers that they could hear each man's groans and whimpers as they carried their burdens to the pile.

"There is something you must have," Dara said.

He pulled a square piece of rosewood from within his robe. It was about two inches long on each side. He handed it to Rick. "You will need this."

The square had two fish carved on one side. On the reverse was a diamond-shaped geometric pattern. It had the same scent of myrrh as the piece the abbot had given Rose.

"You gave something like this to Rose and said the same thing. What do you mean?"

"You are going to do battle with a god. You cannot do that unarmed."

Rick gave the scrap of wood a dismissive look. "This isn't much of a weapon."

"It is far more powerful than you realize. Rosewood has special properties. Treated and blessed as this has been, it can withstand the power of Rudra. It is why the monastery gate was made of rosewood."

"I seem to remember that gate still being destroyed."

"By conventional, not supernatural means. Now we are about to do supernatural combat."

"What do the carvings mean?"

Dara took back the square. "The geometric design is called the endless knot. It has no beginning or end. That symbolizes the endless process of birth, death, and rebirth. It also shows how all things are connected to each other and nothing is separated."

Dara flipped the square over. "The two golden fish consist of a male and female. The fish are portrayed to be standing with their heads facing each other. Like the endless knot, this symbol has Indian roots as representing the prosperous rivers the Ganga and the Yamuna. Now they depict happiness and freedom. But most importantly for us, they show we can live in a state of fearlessness, free of the worry of sinking in the ocean of misery and suffering. That is how you must enter battle. Fearless."

If they were going up against a god, Rick wasn't sure that fearless was really on the menu. "But how will this thing help me?"

"That is up to you." Dara handed the square back to Rick and pointed across the clearing. "Look, it's Charya."

Charya appeared from the jungle where they had first observed the toppled temple. He wandered across the cleared area between the two sets of guards as if he didn't have a care in the world. He whipped a bamboo staff back and forth across the foot-tall weeds as he whistled a tune. The guards might mistake him for an idiot, but certainly not as a threat. Hopefully, that would keep him from being shot on sight.

"Hey, you!" one guard shouted. "Don't you move!"

The not-getting-shot part of the plan had worked. Charya froze mid-whistle and mid swing. He grinned ear-to-ear. "Well, am I glad to see you two! I was afraid I'd be lost out here until I starved to death."

The two guards aimed their rifles in Charya's direction and ran to him. When the slaves saw the guards dash off, they dropped their burdens in unison and collapsed on the ground.

"Now!" Rick said to Dara.

The two bolted for the entrance. As they closed on the seated slaves, several looked up at them. There was no spark of recognition, no smile at the hope of rescue. They were either drugged or had been tortured into some state of hopeless dejection. Rick hoped they could fix that when this was all over.

They made it to the entrance and scrambled down the steps. Oil lamps lit a short hallway and Rick realized in his usual leap-before-looking process, he hadn't even considered bringing light into what had to be darkness. They hurried down the corridor and passed another slave. He did not acknowledge them either. With no hope of rescue, Rick wondered if the slaves just assumed he and Dara were part of Khong's gang. Who else would be out here?

The passage ended at a T-intersection. Rick paused. Neither side looked more promising than the other. His usual method in this kind of equal choice scenario was to go right. He faced in that direction.

"The other way," Dara said. "The Scarlet Heart is in this direction."

Rick wasn't about to argue with the man. They turned left.

But the relief didn't last long. While they passed a number of rooms and blocked passages, there were far more intersections and other passages. Rick was uncomfortably reminded of being in a corn maze. They came to another T-intersection dead end.

"Which way?" Rick said.

Dara looked confused. "I don't know. I sense the Scarlet Heart is straight ahead."

That bit of abbot intuition wasn't any help, and "fake it until you figure it out" wasn't any way to find his wife.

"We need to make a decision," Dara said. "I can feel that the power of the Scarlet Heart is growing."

From down the corridor behind them came Charya's overly loud voice. "I can't tell you what a relief it was seeing you!"

There was another part of the plan Rick hadn't figured on. A captured Charya would be taken into the temple by the same route he and Dara had taken. Now all three of them would become prisoners, if they lived long enough for that to happen.

Rick grabbed Dara by the arm. "Duck in here."

He pulled the abbot into one of the abandoned rooms and they plastered themselves against the walls on either side of the doorway. Charya's voice grew louder as he continued with an unending stream of fawning small talk. Rick knew he was trying to announce his arrival to Rick and Dara. One of the thugs responded with an annoyed grunt, which was followed by a yelp of pain from Charya.

The light through the doorway from the corridor made a pale rectangle on the floor. Footsteps crunched outside the doorway and then three shadows crossed the rectangle of light. Footsteps receded and when Charya spoke again Rick could barely hear him.

"That was close," Dara said.

"Too close," Rick said.

Another problem with this plan they were executing was now crystal clear to Rick. They had two people to rescue.

CHAPTER TWENTY-FIVE

A sharp prod in the kidney from a rifle barrel propelled Charya down the corridor inside the ruined temple. So far, acting the role of the lost fool had kept him from being shot. He doubted it would keep him from being added to the slave labor pool, though. Rick and Dara had better come through for him before that happened.

Charya lost track of all the turns down various passageways he took. The stories of Chraknorok might have been fantastic, but they were true. The rulers had been mining rubies on a massive scale and by the end had honeycombed the ground around the temple with a confusing collection of tunnels. He wondered how the stone-carrying workers he passed managed to find their way out. Then he wondered how he ever could.

"Let's dump him with the other," one of the men said.

His partner agreed and Charya began to worry about how literal the "dumping" part was going to be. He'd always thought that phrase referred to corpses.

Soon the three approached one of Khong's goons standing guard at the doorway to a room. The man looked familiar. Charya winced as he recognized him as one of the men who'd come to get the jade hands from the warehouse. Charya ducked his head to keep his features in shadow and hoped the man had a poor memory.

"Jerry, we found this idiot wandering around outside," Charya's captor said.

Jerry's eyes widened in recognition. It seemed he had a good memory after all. "He's the one who owns that antiques shop in Phnom Penh and tried to steal the hands."

The captor gave Charya a sharp rifle barrel stab in the spine. "So, you was just out on a tour was you?"

"Leave him here," Jerry said, "and notify Tiang. Then get back out there. You can bet he didn't come here alone."

"Heh, maybe Tiang will need a human sacrifice."

The captor shoved Charya past Jerry and into the room. It was about 20 feet square and the hall light didn't illuminate much past the doorway. As Charya righted himself in the center of the room, Rose's voice came from the corner shadows.

"Charya!" Rose stepped out into the light.

Charya was thrilled to see her, and even happier to see that she was unharmed.

"What are you doing here?" she said.

Charya lowered his voice so Jerry couldn't hear him. "Rescuing you and stopping Khong, in that order."

"Becoming a prisoner isn't a good start for either of those." Rose looked past Charya, then whispered, "Where's Rick?"

Charya bent close to Rose's ear and whispered. "He and Dara are in here somewhere. I was the diversion."

"What's their plan to get us out of here?"

Charya wrinkled his forehead. "Well, we really didn't think that far ahead. Kind of play-it-by-ear once they got past the guards."

"That sounds like one of Rick's plans, all right. Never think when you can act first."

"We did consider we were in a bit of a race against time."

"Well, you were right there. Tiang and Khong have the statue reassembled and Tiang is doing some sort of ritual to prepare it for Rudra's transfer into me."

"Rick and Dara will find a way to keep that from happening."

"My husband has a penchant for picking long shot winners at the track," Rose said. "I hope he's saved a little of that luck for today."

Tiang appeared in the doorway, panting hard with sweat across his brow. One of Khong's armed thugs stood behind him. Tiang made a growling noise, charged in and gripped Charya by the neck. "Who else is here with you?"

"A company of colonial troops are surrounding Chraknorok right now," Charya croaked out. "You had better escape while you can."

Instead of the statement stoking fear in Tiang, he smiled and released Charya. "Khong has the colonial forces paid off at every level, and they would never venture this deep into the jungle anyway. That means it's just you and the other American. One Westerner against Khong's gang and the power of Rudra. He has no chance."

"Rick has a habit of beating the odds," Rose said.

"Not today. He's too late. We are ready to start the ritual." Tiang turned to Jerry. "Keep an eye on the shopkeeper. I'm taking her to the Chamber of Rebirth."

"It's finally time?" Jerry said.

"Yes, and when it's done, the shopkeeper can have the honor of being Rudra's first victim."

***

Rose was afraid that Tiang was right, and that Rick's rescue attempt would be far too little and far too late.

The guard smiled and seemed to take relish in manhandling Rose out of her makeshift prison cell. The other goon and Rose followed Tiang back through the passageway maze. As soon as they entered the antechamber to the Chamber of Rebirth, dread hit Rose like a pile driver. She was out of time. Rick and Dara weren't coming, and Rudra was.

She did have one hope. She slid her hand in her pocket and cupped it around the rosewood disc. Dara had said she'd need this. Rose doubted he just meant having it to scratch the equivalent of Hansel's breadcrumb trail on the passageway walls. Whatever this disc was supposed to do, it was going to have to do it damn soon.

The images on the anteroom walls of Rudra wielding her destructive power sickened Rose. All of that was about to come to pass again, but this time everyone would see Rudra doing it from within Rose's body. The monster the world would fear and despise would be her.

They entered the Chamber of Rebirth. There were twice as many burning lamps as the last time and the room was well-lit in flickering yellow. The Rudra statue had been fully restored. Four large incense burners surrounded the statue and the air had a sweet, floral aroma. The jade hands glowed green as if they had lights inside them. A chain with manacles at each end had been draped across the hands and the ends dangled about five feet from the floor. On its forehead, the Scarlet Heart ruby pulsed red with the unnerving regularity of a heartbeat. Most bizarre were the eyes, which Rose was certain were carved into the stone. Now they glowed a deep red.

But Rose didn't need all those physical cues to know that Rudra was closer to being released. She could feel the demonic god's presence. The air in the room felt oppressively heavy. The scent of sulphur seared her nose. She felt a gnawing hunger and angry anticipation, but those emotions weren't hers, they were Rudra's, emanating from within the statue. The god seethed within the stone, like a pacing lion awaiting its cage door to open.

Khong had a different seat this time. His sedan chair was front row and centered on Rudra's statue. It seemed he didn't want to miss a moment of the ritual.

Neither did a large number of the mercenaries. Over a dozen sat scattered in the amphitheater seats. Rose guessed that the slave labor had been halted and the workers left under guard so the rest of the gang could watch Rudra's return, and Rose's own demise.

Tiang grabbed Rose under one armpit and frog-marched her down the steps. At the halfway point, the statue's eyes glowed a brighter red and the amphitheater rumbled.

Tiang smiled. Then he dragged Rose the rest of the way until she stood beside the chains that dangled from Rudra's hands. Tiang clamped the manacles around her wrists. That left her hands uncomfortably above her head. She wouldn't last long standing like this, but if Rudra possessed her, she wouldn't have to.

Tiang stepped back and took a deep breath and seemed to be savoring this moment of impending victory.

"What are you waiting for?" Khong shouted from behind him. "Get on with it."

The mercenaries in the amphitheater cheered their support for their boss.

Tiang grimaced and his face flushed. Rose thought if Tiang had his way, Khong would be the first victim of Rudra's wrath. Maybe that had been Tiang's plan all along.

Tiang circumnavigated the statue, lighting the four incense burners as he did. Rose recognized the scent in an instant as the same one she'd spilled during the thug's attack in the antiques shop. When he'd finished lighting the last one, he resumed his place before the statue and began a chant in a language Rose did not understand.

But Rudra certainly understood. The statue's eyes and hands grew brighter. The manacles that bound Rose warmed. She looked up to see that the chain links touching the hands glowed the same jade green color. Link by link, the color crept down the chains on both sides.

The oppressive presence that had tainted the room since she stepped in grew stronger. The raspy voice she'd heard earlier returned. Between heavy, growling pants it said "Surrender and save yourself the agony."

Rose wasn't about to surrender. She clenched her fists and prepared for a mental fight. She'd keep Rudra out for as long as possible, and hope that Rick and a rescue party arrived before she succumbed.

CHAPTER TWENTY-SIX

Rick's heart pounded as he struggled to decide which path to take in the underground maze. Only one way could get him to Rose.

Then Rick noticed a mark etched on the wall. The letter R had been drawn in some kind of reddish material. Flakes of the material were fresh on the wall and on the floor below. Rick knelt to examine it and caught the scent of myrrh. The color matched the rosewood medallion Dara had given Rose and the one he had in his pocket.

Rick's heart skipped a beat. Rose had drawn an R for Rick to get his attention. The other side of the wall contained a short line, but as far as Rick was concerned, that was as good as an arrow. Rose had left them trail markers. Her rosewood disc had come in handy after all.

That's my Rosie, Rick thought.

"Dara, look," Rick said. "Rose marked the way for us."

Dara knelt and examined the mark. He touched it with one finger. "Myrrh-infused rosewood. Your wife is very clever."

Around the corner was another small mark, just a line. But as far as Rick was concerned it might as well have been a neon sign. "This way."

Dara followed Rick down the passageway. Rick kept his eye out for more rosewood marks at what would be thigh-high for Rose, the most unobtrusive height to casually scrape the wall. At intersection after intersection, he found and followed the marks. What he didn't find along the way were any more of Khong's gang or any slave laborers.

"Not to jinx us," Rick said, "but we've been pretty lucky not being discovered by any of Khong's men."

"It isn't luck," Dara said. "I can sense that the ritual has started. They are all likely watching it."

"Then we'd better hurry."

***

In the Chamber of Rebirth, Rose's shoulders ached from having her arms chained above her head. In front of her, Tiang closed his eyes, moved his arms to his sides, and faced his palms down. His hands sent waves of energy downward and Tiang levitated off the ground. Through that he continued to repeat his chant, with his voice growing deeper and more guttural with every repetition. The statue's glowing eyes became brighter and when Tiang stopped and hovered before Rudra's face, they lit his entire body in a rich red, as if he'd been coated in blood.

The crowd in the room went silent, but more than that. They also went still, frozen in place. They were more than mesmerized though. It was as if time had stopped for them. Rose wasn't even sure if they were breathing.

The glow lit more of the links of the chain that bound Rose until it finally touched the manacles. The manacles grew so hot Rose was sure they would burn her skin. Overhead, rock ground and crumbled as the corners of the mouth on the Rudra statue turned up into a malevolent smile.

Below the floating Tiang and in front of Rose, Rudra appeared. Nine feet tall, skin a bright blue, with four arms and a snarl on her face. Her eyes glowed as red as the statue above her. She opened her mouth and revealed rows of shark-like teeth.

Tiang, with his eyes closed in concentration, did not react. Neither did Khong or the mercenaries in the amphitheater seats, locked as they were in some kind of paralysis. All of that made Rose feel like she was alone with the resurrected god. A fear more overwhelming than any she'd experienced coursed through every vein in Rose's body.

"My vessel is delivered," Rudra said.

That statement inspired enough anger for Rose to shake off her fear. "I will never be your vessel."

"You act like you have a choice. You have been prepared. Your body will be taken. Your essence will be erased."

Rose knew she needed to buy Rick more time. "You failed the last time you tried to enter our reality. You will fail this time as well."

"All cycles do not repeat. Aberrations are corrected. Jayavarman's false religion should never have taken hold. I should never have been exiled to that prison reality. My return should not have been thwarted. All of these aberrations will be corrected moments from now when Tiang's incantation is complete."

"You're in for a fight," Rose said.

Rudra laughed. "So said the ant to the sole of a sandal. A puff of my breath is all it will take to erase you. Can't you feel my power growing as the ritual goes on?"

Rose had hoped that was just her imagination working overtime. There was no denying that the more Tiang chanted, the brighter the glow from the statue's face became, and the stronger and more terrifying Rudra felt. It was like Tiang was slowly opening a valve and letting super-heated steam escape, and Rose was about to be scalded.

"Do you think I would have selected you from all of humanity if you were not destined to be my vessel? From the moment the jade hand went missing, to the fool in America finding it and giving it to you, to your 'accidental' preparation in the antique store, all of this has been guided by me. Your service as my vessel is an inescapable fate."

Tiang finished one chant with a shout. The tops of the four incense burners blew off and bounced off the ceiling. All four spouted a deep red flame Rose had never seen in any fire. A blanket of sulphur-infused air fell over the room.

Rudra smiled, stepped forward, and held Rose's head in her two upper hands. Despite their icy-blue color, they felt hot as branding irons. Rose screamed.

Then Rudra's lower hands reared back and plunged into Rose's chest. Not by breaking the skin and sending fountains of blood everywhere, but by passing through the skin and ribs, as if Rose were a ghost. Both hands wrapped around her heart. Searing pain surrounded her heart like it had been set afire. It stopped beating.

Using Rose's heart as an anchor, Rudra pulled herself forward and passed fully into Rose's body. The physical and mental anguish of coexistence with monstrous evil blanked out all her senses. Rose screamed and knew no rescue was coming.

***

The sound of Rose's scream sent a chill up Rick's spine. "That's Rosie!"

He bolted past Dara and down the passageway in the direction of her cry. It had sounded very close. At the next intersection he glimpsed a rosewood mark and followed it left. The passageway opened to a wider, taller hall with walls covered in murals of Rudra the Destroyer in action. At the far end, a doorway led to a much brighter room.

Rick knew Rose was in that room.

He ran to that last opening and stopped as he crossed the threshold. The stink of sulphur polluted the air. A sense of dread hit him so hard he had to grab the threshold for support.

He stood at the top of a semicircular auditorium of some kind. Down where the stage would be stood a huge statue of Rudra. In front of it, Tiang floated about ten feet off the ground, illuminated by the red glow of the statue's eyes and the Scarlet Heart affixed to the statue's forehead.

But all that mattered was Rose cuffed in a chain that ran across the statue's jade hands. Her arms were raised over her head and she had a heartbreaking look of anguish on her face. Rick launched himself for the stairs down to his wife.

Dara's hand grabbed him at the shoulder and stopped him. "Wait. Look."

The abbot's command was impossible to resist. Rick paused. The seats had dozens of Khong's men in them, He hadn't noticed because they looked frozen stiff, like statues among the broken stones that still littered the amphitheater.

"Rudra has frozen the unbelievers in the Chamber of Rebirth. Even Khong, that fat man in the sedan chair down front, sits there as one already dead. But they are not. They are just suspended in time, caught in the disturbance of the rip between our reality and Rudra's. This is one of the reasons Chraknorok's soldiers were so easily defeated by King Jayavarman. All those at the ritual were incapacitated. Enter and the same will happen to you."

"But Rose is down there, in pain. Rudra must be attacking her."

"She is. And I will stop her. Tiang is my failure. I must put an end to his evil acts."

"Can you?"

Dara slipped his arm from the sling made of his purple sash. He took it from his neck and retied it around his waist. "I am still the abbot of Phenum Aoral monastery, Tiang is still a failed initiate, and karma is in our favor."

Rick thought that trusting Rose's life to karma was worse than betting the shop on a hot tip from a bookie. "I'll go with you."

Dara laid his hand on Rick's chest. "This is not your time. Wait here. Rose will need you when I am finished."

Rick didn't like Dara using the word finished. It sounded far too final, like the sign announcing a dead end.

"I need a moment to prepare." Dara closed his eyes and folded his hands before his face. He repeated a series of phrases in an unintelligible whisper, then raised his head and opened his eyes. "Now it is the beginning of the end. Which of course will be a new beginning."

Rick stepped back into the anteroom. Dara began a slow procession down the steps to the Rudra statue. Rick hoped the old man knew what he was doing. If not, it was going to end up being Rick against a room full of Khong's thugs and a vengeful Vedic goddess.

CHAPTER TWENTY-SEVEN

As he levitated before the statue of Rudra, Tiang finished the final line of the incantation and exhaled with relief.

But something was wrong. Rudra had not finished possessing the woman. The goddess was making progress, but the resurrection was not quite complete. How could this properly prepared, Western woman be putting up such a strong fight?

He sensed something else was wrong. An unwanted presence had spoiled the hall, a presence Tiang was far too familiar with.

Tiang rotated around. His eyebrows arched as he saw Dara standing halfway down the center steps. Tiang could not believe it. He remembered how much he hated this hide-bound old man. Tiang hovered forward to over the bottom of the steps where Dara stood.

"I thought I'd killed you back at the monastery," he said.

"As with your education there," Dara said, "you left the job unfinished."

"A so-called education where your initiates learn nothing that really matters. You teach them to live in terror of great power, instead of embracing it."

Dara resumed descending the steps. "We dedicated our lives to protecting the world from the power of evil, the darkness of anger and hatred, the belief that death is more important than life."

"Rudra understands that without death, there can be no new life. As a snake sheds its skin and is renewed, so mankind must experience a mass extinction to be reborn better than before."

Dara scoffed. "And you think that Rudra speaks to you? That she chose as a confidant not the heads of nations, not religious leaders, but a psychopath who has failed at everything he has attempted?"

"Look behind me," Tiang said. "Rudra is reborn in a new body. Does that look like failure?"

"It looks like all things you start, unfinished."

Tiang seethed. He knew the damned abbot was right. Rudra's resurrection remained incomplete. Closer yet, but still incomplete. *What was it about this woman that was making it so hard?*

"There is one bit of business I can finish right now." Tiang closed his fists and dropped to the floor. He landed and took a knee. He could not suppress a wicked grin as he raised both palms in Dara's direction. Then he sent two compression pulses straight at Dara.

The old man didn't flinch. Tiang could not wait to see the charges shred the abbot to pieces.

The two pulses struck Dara square in the chest. But then passed through him and blasted the steps behind him. Stone exploded and chunks struck and killed two of the mercenaries sitting nearby. They died without a sound and their corpses toppled over with the grace of a falling store mannequin.

"This can't be," Tiang said.

"In your ignorance you don't know what decades of mental discipline can harvest. Lying on beds of nails and walking across hot coals are only a start. Your power caught me unaware at the monastery. But now I am prepared. Your compression waves can pass right through me."

Tiang's failure made him furious. He pulled a long knife from a scabbard on his belt. "I bet I can make this pass through you, but you won't be standing after I do."

"This is your last chance to repent and leave the path of shadows and return to the path of light. Before Rudra is resurrected, the two of us can send her back."

"Old man, I shouldn't kill you so I can watch you writhe after Rudra's return. But I'm too excited to feel you exhale your last breath to exercise that kind of restraint."

Tiang charged up the steps at Dara with his knife held high. They met and Dara deflected the blow, grabbed Tiang's arm, and flipped him over Dara's head. Tiang landed hard on the steps, but managed to not break anything. He rolled over and jumped to his feet.

So, the old man still has a few tricks from his early days as a warrior monk, Tiang thought. *But he is still an old, unarmed man. No amount of mental training will overcome that.*

Tiang rushed Dara again, this time with the knife held low. They clashed and began a dance of thrust and parry as Tiang tried to plunge the blade into his former mentor. He noticed Dara wince as his right forearm blocked a blow, then saw that the abbot was favoring that whole right side. Tiang realized his opportunity.

Tiang made a sloppy thrust to Dara's left side. As the abbot twisted to avoid the blade, Tiang sent a crashing blow into Dara's right shoulder with his left fist.

Dara moaned and staggered back. Tiang lunged and sent another blow to Dara's vulnerable shoulder. This time the old man cried out.

"Where's that mental discipline you were bragging about?" Tiang struck a third time at Dara's shoulder. The abbot went down on one knee. Tiang placed the sharp edge of his blade against the abbot's neck. "Just like back at the monastery, you can't accept the narrow limits of your power."

"And you still don't accept the intervention of karma."

Overhead, the ceiling made a sharp, loud cracking noise. Tiang looked up just as a piano-sized chunk fell away. He dove right, but the piece was too large to escape. He hit the ground between two seats as the ceiling section crashed down on him. The world faded to black and he cursed karma for the final time.

***

Rick had seen the lopsided fight between Tiang and Dara and had followed instructions and not intervened. The ceiling collapse changed that in a hurry. If Rudra was going to turn him into a statue for trying to save Rose, so be it.

He ran down the steps between the motionless mercenaries. At every step he was sure one of them would reach out and grab him. But none of them moved.

He did not freeze, didn't even feel anything trying to slow him down. What he did feel was the square in his pocket getting warmer with every step he took down. Perhaps something about it was keeping Rudra's spell at bay, or maybe it had been Tiang's spell, now less powerful with him on the sidelines. Rick only cared about the result, not the reason. He stopped short at the debris from the ceiling.

Tiang lay on his back with a huge section of the ceiling pinning him from the chest down. Rick couldn't tell if he was breathing and didn't care as he jumped on and then over the slab to tend to Dara. He landed and then knelt at the abbot's side.

The majority of the ceiling collapse had missed him save for smaller chunks of rock and dust. What hadn't missed him was Tiang's knife. It protruded from Dara's chest. Pain twisted Dara's face.

Rick reached for the knife. "I'll get it out."

Dara pushed him away with his good hand. "Get Rose first."

Rick sprang to his feet and then up on the dais. Rose hung limp in the manacles, head bowed, eyes closed. Rick feared the worst.

He stepped forward and grabbed her under the arms. He lifted her up to take the weight off her wrists. Rose raised her head. Her eyes opened, unfocused and dull.

"Rosie! Am I glad to see you. Let's get you out of those manacles and far away from here as fast as possible."

Rose didn't respond. She just stared at Rick.

"Rose?"

Rose's eyes turned to a glowing red. Her flaccid muscles beneath his hands turned hard as steel.

In a voice that sounded nothing like Rick's wife she said, "Rose is gone forever."

CHAPTER TWENTY-EIGHT

Terrified and repulsed, Rick dropped Rose like she was on fire.

But she did not fall. She remained floating. Her mouth split into a grin that was more serpentine than any Rose could ever make, and Rick knew that Rudra had possessed his wife's body. With a flick of her wrists, she snapped the chain where it hung up between the jade hands and both sections cascaded down to the floor in a stereo crash.

Rick retreated up the nearest set of steps to the top of the amphitheater. Then he remembered what Dara had said about being strong in the face of evil. Rudra was just using Rose's body as a macabre mask. He stopped and turned around. Rick focused on Rudra's wicked smile, the most un-Rose-like attribute the goddess displayed.

This isn't Rose, he thought. *But it will be again when I send this thing packing.*

"Kneel, pathetic mortal," Rudra said. "Be the first to worship your returning goddess."

Rick took another step back. "To be fair, all the guys in here were in line ahead of me. I'll wait and go after them."

"You dare mock an immortal, you worthless flesh bag? Then die with the rest of them."

Rudra raised her hands and sent a set of shockwaves across the room. They struck Khong first. His head jerked back like the hinged top on a beer stein. His arms snapped straight out from his sides. Twin beams of intense white light shot from his eyes and seared two black circles in the ceiling. The light cut off and Khong's body went limp. In the place of his eyes were two smoking, blackened sockets.

As the shockwave struck each row of frozen gangsters, each man's arms snapped up at his sides and his head rolled back to an impossible angle. Then like two tiny searchlights, intense beams blasted from their eyes. When it faded, the corpses dropped to the floor.

Before Rick could run from the shockwave, it hit him. He braced for his imminent, awful death.

It did not come. Light beams had burst from every thug in the chamber, but Rick remained unaffected. The wave rolled to the end of the room and faded against the far wall.

Rick could not explain how this deliverer of death had passed him by. Then he felt the rosewood square vibrating in his back pocket and feeling so hot he thought it would have burned bare skin. The abbot's gift had protected him from Rudra's paralysis and the force she'd used to slaughter the others in the room.

Rudra's eyes widened at the sight of Rick still standing. "How can you still be alive? That wave should have killed all but the religious elect."

"That apple-a-day thing is really paying off for me. The real joke is on you. You just killed everyone who was going to help you seize power."

Rudra laughed. It was a vicious, malevolent laugh that Rose could not have affected even if she tried. "Do you think I need these worthless mortals to conquer the world? All your militaries cannot stop me. This room full of fools were just a means to an end."

Rick wished Khong and Tiang were alive to hear that.

"Somehow you can resist the power of my compression wave," Rudra continued, "but you can't resist the power of gravity. How about being buried alive?"

Rudra angled both palms to a spot near Rick's feet. Narrow streams of compression waves streaked from her and into the spot on the ground. Stone vaporized. The waves then started to excavate a hole. As it deepened it expanded, it headed for Rick at a rate he'd never outrun. Once he tumbled in, Rudra would collapse more of the temple on top of him. He wasn't going to get out of this temple alive.

The compression waves stopped. Rudra turned her palms inward until they faced each other.

"What is happening?" The shock in her voice was profound.

Compression waves shot from both hands. They struck each other in the center. An explosion detonated like a thunderclap. The force blew Rudra back against one leg of her statue. Rick caught sight of the disc Dara had given Rose glowing in her pocket.

Rick's heart swelled. His Rosie was still in there, still fighting.

Dara had explained the meaning of the two golden fish. Now Rick truly understood what they represented. The fish were the two of them, fearless in the face of Rudra, linked through the sacred discs.

Rick jumped over the hole in the ground and ran up onto the dais. Rudra growled, jumped forward, and sent a compression wave up at the ceiling over his head. Stone shattered and rained down. Rick jumped left and just dodged the downpour. He stood only feet from Rudra.

"Okay, Rosie," he said, looking straight at Rudra. "I know you're in there. She knows you're in there. And you're scaring the hell out of her."

"I fear no mortal," Rudra said.

"I know a bluff when I see one," Rick said. "And that was the worst one ever. You picked the wrong vessel for sure. Boy, it's hard to believe that in all your time among humans you never learned that you don't want to tangle with an angry redhead."

"Drive me out and Rose will die, just like Jayavarman's queen."

"My guess is that the queen died when you possessed her," Rick said. "Her love for her king wasn't enough to anchor her in our reality and keep her alive. You bet against Rose and I being soulmates. You're about to lose that bet."

Rudra snarled and raised a hand at Rick. Rick whipped the rosewood square from his pocket and held it up. The block glowed pink.

"C'mon, Rosie," he said. "Meet me halfway."

Rudra's hand trembled. Then her entire arm shook. Muscles tensed as Rose and Rudra fought for control. Slowly, jerkily, Rudra's arm returned to her side. She screamed in frustration. The goddess started to lunge for Rick, but only got one foot forward before she stopped as if her other foot was glued to the ground. Rudra wailed in a pitch that made Rick's ears hurt.

Rick stepped closer to Rudra. It was like wading through evil. The air felt thick, and a primal, indescribable fear threatened to send him fleeing. His subconscious knew that whatever he was approaching could kill him. His conscious mind hoped there was enough Rose in control that it wouldn't happen.

Rudra's head jerked back and forth, as if trying to shake something free. Rick knew what that was. That was Rosie beating this goddess at her own game of possession.

Rick put the rosewood back in his pocket and stepped right up to Rudra. She reeked of sulphur. The goddess hissed at him and her breath stank of carrion. Rick fought back his revulsion and the horror of it all coming from something that looked like Rose. He grabbed the chains that still hung from Rudra's manacles and swung them around behind the statue's leg. He caught the ends as they came around and then tied them together across Rudra's chest. He tightened the knot and pinned her to the statue.

If Rudra used the chains to get into Rose, he hoped that Rose could use the chains to push her back out. Then he grabbed Rudra's shoulders and pressed her back against the statue's leg. He stared into her red eyes. Rudra growled like a wild cat.

"C'mon Rosie. I'm right here. I've got her on the outside. You get her from the inside."

The rosewood pieces in both Rick and Rose's pockets glowed brighter. Rudra growled and reached for hers. Rick pinned her arm harder to the statue.

Rudra resisted. She was stronger than Rose had ever been. Without the chain's help, Rick was sure he could not have held her. Even with the chains, he was beginning to have his doubts.

Rudra stopped struggling. "No! Not again. I'm not going back there!"

Rudra screamed. The shackles around her wrists glowed green. That glow moved to the chains, then to the leg of the statue, then it faded away. Rudra's eyes rolled up in her head, then closed. Her body went limp. Rudra's head drooped until her chin touched her chest.

The two rosewood pieces cooled and went dark.

Rick's first, fearful thought was of the Cambodian queen dying as Rudra left her body. He released his grip on Rose's shoulders and cupped her chin in one hand.

"Rosie? Wake up and talk to me. Please."

Her eyelids fluttered open and revealed the beautiful blue eyes Rick had fallen in love with at first sight.

"Rick," Rose whispered. "I'm back."

Rick kissed her hard on the lips and then hugged her as well as the chains and statue would permit. "I knew you'd do it. No goddess has a chance against my Rosie."

"It was touch and go there," she said. "But I knew the two of us could do it."

Rick untied the chain and helped Rose stand away from the statue. He looked up just as the last glow of the hands, eyes and the Scarlet Heart faded away.

"Looks like we sent her packing," Rick said.

"Don't kid yourself," said a voice from the amphitheater.

Rick and Rose whirled around. Tiang had both hands under the stone slab that pinned him to the ground. With little effort, he flipped it off himself and across the room.

Tiang stood up. His clothes were bloody and the fallen stone had to have broken most of the bones in the man's body. But somehow he was able to stand there like nothing had happened. Tiang stared at the two of them and Rick knew how he'd managed it.

Tiang's eyes glowed red.

CHAPTER TWENTY-NINE

Tiang's possession shocked Rose. In her fight with the evil goddess, she'd been certain her essence had been driven back into the statue.

"Did you two think a pair of cheap talismans would be enough to defeat a goddess?" Rudra said.

"Tiang said he wasn't prepared, couldn't be possessed," Rose said to Rick.

Rudra answered anyway. "Couldn't *safely* be possessed. The body will last long enough for me to kill the two of you and find another."

"Our talismans protect us from your power," Rick said. "You've seen that."

"But that's all they protect you from."

Rudra stepped down closer to the stage. As she did, she spread her arms and sent two compression waves into the rubble. Two huge stones rose from the debris. They hovered and then aligned with Rick and Rose.

Rudra was right. Rose had seen bits of falling ceiling strike Rick. The talismans might protect them from the supernatural, but that was all. These blocks would smash them flat.

Rudra's eyes flashed brighter and the corners of her lips swept up in a devilish smile.

Then she screamed.

Both stones dropped to the ground with a thunderous crash. Rudra collapsed, revealing Dara standing cockeyed behind her. Rudra fell forward with the knife that had impaled Dara sticking out of her back. The handle was wrapped in Dara's purple sash.

Dara dropped to his knees. Fresh blood gushed from his chest wound.

Rick and Rose ran past Rudra to the abbot. He leaned back against the steps and held up a hand.

"Finish her," he said.

Rose checked Rudra. Indeed, what should have been a fatal stab wound had not been. She had reached around, pulled the knife free, and lay on the floor facing them.

"My force of will can keep the dead alive long enough to kill all of you."

Dara's voice was little more than a whisper. "Use the talismans."

Rose took hers out of her pocket and it began to glow again. Rick did the same. Rudra recoiled. Rose suddenly knew what to do. She slammed her talisman hard against Rudra's chest. The goddess cried out and then Rick pressed his against the goddess as well. Together they pushed her hard against the floor.

Both talismans burst into a light so brilliant it flash-blinded Rose. She was shocked that no heat or sound accompanied the burst. When her vision cleared, she and Rick were kneeling over Tiang's body. His eyes were clear and lifeless, his arms splayed out at his sides. Where she and Rick had held the talismans, all that remained of them were piles of reddish ash.

Rick and Rose hugged in relief and Rick kissed her hard.

"Imagine a goddess thinking she could beat us," Rick said.

They scrambled over to Dara. The old man was breathing hard. Rick took the sash from the knife on the steps and wrapped it into a compress. He placed it over Dara's wound.

"How badly are you hurt?" Rick said.

"Not enough to kill me," Dara said. "I hope. The knife didn't go deep and didn't seem to hit anything vital."

"Looks like we killed Rudra, though," Rick said.

"You cannot kill a goddess."

"Well, whatever you did to those talismans sent her running."

"All I did was link the talismans. You powered them to send her back to her prison reality. You should be proud. King Jayavarman needed a half-dozen abbots to do the same thing."

"How could a knife stab a goddess?" Rose said.

"It did not," Dara said. "It stabbed the unprepared body the goddess possessed. Only a purified and prepared body can have all the goddess' powers."

Charya's voice came from the Chamber of Rebirth entrance. "I thought I'd never find you. What did I miss?"

"Evil goddess came," Rick said, "and evil goddess went."

"How did you get past the goon guarding you?" Rose said.

"A mob of the forced laborers came charging down the passageway and ran him off."

"They must have taken advantage of having most of Khong's men in the Chamber of Rebirth," Rick said. "Come help me get Dara out of here."

"No," Rose said. "I'll do that. Charya, you need to disassemble that statue again and separate the hands and the Scarlet Heart of Kymer. We don't want to go through all this again."

Dara offered a weak smile. "If fighting Rudra this time doesn't kill me, the next time surely will."

"I'll get on it," Charya said. He headed for a ladder propped against the wall behind the dais.

Rick and Rose draped one of Dara's arms over each of their shoulders and helped him up the steps and into the antechamber. He promised he could walk from there.

Rose didn't believe him, but she and Rick let him stand on his own anyway. They headed down the chamber between the rows of log supports.

"Tell us more about those rosewood talismans you gave us," Rick said.

"They were left to the monastery by the first abbot. They were carved and carried into battle by the monks who first repelled Rudra. What those monks did to initially enchant the talismans has been lost to time."

"But their power certainly wasn't," Rick said.

"I have spent most of my life around them. They have never been that powerful. I believe they were conductors of energy. Hundreds of years ago, it was the power of the assembled abbots. Today it was the power of the bond you two have."

"That's what it felt like to me," Rose said.

"Same here," Rick said.

As they approached the other side of the antechamber, Charya entered from the Chamber of Rebirth and ran to catch up to them. He had an old rice sack over one shoulder. "I have all three items. I can't believe how easily they came off the statue."

"Rudra's power is too weak to hold them in place," Dara said, "at least for now. She is back in her prison reality. She will recover, and be awaiting the next group of fools who will try to set her free."

"Then it's important that we disperse everything in that bag far and wide," Rose said.

"And since the statue can't be destroyed," Rick said, "somehow make Chraknorok undiscovered again."

The sound of an advancing crowd came from the anteroom entrance. Then a group of now-liberated laborers poured through the door. They had vengeful looks on their faces, but as soon as they saw the abbot in his robe, they passed around the four of them like a river around a boulder. As they passed, Rose saw each was carrying sticks of dynamite.

Charya stopped one and they exchanged a few lines of conversation before the man hurried on his way.

"One problem is solved," Charya said. "The laborers freed themselves, killed or ran off the few remaining thugs in the city, and then ransacked the excavation supplies. They plan to blast and collapse this entire temple complex."

Rose looked over at the amazing anteroom artwork on the walls depicting Rudra's rule. This place was evil incarnate and had to be destroyed. But for a few seconds, the history-loving part of her lamented the loss of these amazing creations.

As they stood there, a laborer went to a nearby log ceiling support and tied three sticks of dynamite to it. He then affixed a long fuse.

"That's our cue to go," Rick said. "I have a feeling they won't wait for us to send this place tumbling down."

The four made their way out of the ruins as fast as Dara could manage.

"Your clues were brilliant," Rick said to Rose. "I saw the letter R you etched on the wall. You knew R for Rick would catch my attention."

Rose sighed. "That was R for Rose you idiot, the person you were looking for."

"Yes, of course. Just kidding."

They paused at the city's edge. Soon laborers came streaming out of the ruins like ants from a kicked anthill. Just as the last few escaped, a series of underground detonations boomed. The ground shook beneath Rose's feet. Streams of dirt and dust blasted from a number of entrances around the ruins. The remains of the main temple expanded like a balloon getting its first puffs of air.

Then the entire complex collapsed inward. It was as if the ground had opened up and swallowed it. A mushroom-shaped cloud of dust billowed up through the trees. When the dust cleared, the ground was practically level. At a distance, the former city would look like a clearing in the forest. At the rate things grew around here, Rose figured that in a year it wouldn't even look like that.

"King Jayavarman's army gave Chraknorok a good pummeling," Charya said, "but they can't hold a candle to kidnapped Cambodians seeking revenge."

"How do we get home from here?" Rose asked.

"We have a boat." Rick knit his brow. "Uh, one of you can find our way back to the boat, can't you?"

"Of course," Charya said.

"I have a feeling Guo will be surprised to see us come back," Rick said.

"Even more surprised when we don't," Charya said. "I think we'll just travel down the Mekong all the way to Phom Penh and home. I, for one, could use a relaxing boat ride."

CHAPTER THIRTY

One day later

The docks at Phnom Penh were a welcome sight. After a full day sitting inside the little boat, Rose was ready to go ashore, get clean, and go home.

"We're going to skip a public arrival at the docks," Charya said. "Too many prying eyes would lead to too many questions. There is also a good chance Guo will have people on the lookout for us since we have neither returned this boat nor given him the location of Chraknorok."

Charya turned toward a clump of trees on the western riverbank. "Instead, I'll beach the boat north of the docks at that overgrown place."

"How will you get your truck back?" Rick said.

"I won't, but I wouldn't have anyway. Guo probably sold it as soon as we left his office."

He beached the boat and everyone got out and walked to the main road. Rose's concern about walking all the way to the city proved to be unjustified. Within minutes, a stake bed truck offered them a ride. Well, the driver offered saffron-robed monk Dara a ride, and Dara made the man bring them all. Dara's abbot's robes seemed to open doors. Soon they were back in Charya's shop with the rice sack filled with artifacts on the counter. The four circled it in silence.

"Now we have the dilemma about what to do with these," Charya said as he pointed to the sack.

"Dara's monks took care of the Scarlet Heart for centuries," Rick said. "Seems right up their alley to handle them."

"And through my arrogance about that divine mission," Dara said, "I lost the Scarlet Heart and Rudra was resurrected, however briefly." He nodded across the counter at Rick and Rose. "You should take them."

"Us?" Rick said.

"No, just her."

That assignment startled Rose. "Me?"

"You stood up to Rudra toe-to-toe. No one better to trust these with. You two will take them out of the country with you now. Neither I nor Charya will know where they are. Anyone who decides to embark on a new Rudra resurrection folly will be Cambodian, and the trail in Cambodia will be a dead end. I can trust you to hide these where they will not be found."

"I can do that," Rose said.

Dara slid the bag in her direction. "Then get back to your plane and get started."

***

Charya arranged for a ride to get Rick and Rose back to their plane. They were both thrilled to find it and Humphrey both in one piece. They met the pilot under the wing and Rose gave him a condensed version of what they'd been through.

"Rick, it wasn't no picnic here, you know. You wouldn't believe what happened. I got attacked by ghost monkeys."

Rose raised an eyebrow in disbelief. "Monkey ghosts?"

"No, not the ghosts of monkeys. Monkeys with ghosts inside them. They came and stole my tools and the gasket material. I followed them back to a haunted plantation."

"Humphrey, stop kidding around and let's just get out of here."

"Rick, I ain't kidding. Then them monkeys attacked me and I thought for sure I was a goner until a tiger came out of nowhere and saved my butt."

"Knock it off, okay? I appreciate you being able to get the plane back in the air. It wasn't as dangerous as what we did, but it was pretty damn important."

"Aw, Rick, I ain't joshing—"

A shout came from across the field. "*Arrêtez cet avion!*"

At the edge of the field, a short Frenchman in a pith helmet wearing a narrow tie pointed at the plane. An official-looking badge hung on his shirt pocket. A soldier beside him had a rifle slung over one shoulder.

"We've officially overstayed our welcome," Rick said.

"We couldn't stay hidden from the Frenchies forever," Humphrey said.

The three of them climbed into the plane. Rick and Humphrey scrambled forward into the pilot seats. Rose took a passenger seat in the rear. Up front, switches clicked as Rick and Humphrey readied the engines to start.

On the seat beside Rose lay a copy of the Savannah newspaper. A lemon-shaped hole had been cut through several pages. That hole looked the same size and shape as the base of the leaking oil pump Humphrey had shown them.

Humphrey had said that monkeys had taken his gasket material. He didn't say that he'd gotten it back. Rose grabbed the paper and went to the cockpit.

"If you didn't have gasket material," Rose said to Humphrey, "what did you make a gasket out of?"

Humphrey looked sheepish. "Something just as good, don't you worry."

Rose waved the cut-out newspaper pages in his face. "Something like the funny papers?"

Rick blanched. "Humphrey, you didn't make a gasket out of newspaper, did you?"

"Naw, that would be plumb stupid. I made it out of newspaper and rubber."

"Where did you get rubber?"

"From a rubber tree."

"You mean rubber sap?" Rose said. "That's not the same as rubber. It has to be heated and vulcanized to become rubber."

"Once the engine heats up, that's just what it's gonna do. I think."

"You *think* so?" Rose said.

"Humphrey's been keeping this plane together for years," Rick said adding a dismissive wave. "He knows what he's doing."

Rose was about to rebut that statement with a long list of exceptions when the French official shouted at them from outside the plane. Now he stood a few feet from the nose, and the soldier beside him had his rifle off his shoulder.

Humphrey hit the starter and the center engine coughed and cranked to life. He whipped the throttle up. The instant breeze sent the French official and the soldier staggering backward.

"You'd better grab a seat, Rosie," Rick said.

Rose threw the newspaper down in disgust and took a seat in the back just as the starboard engine cranked up. It belched out a cloud of black smoke. Rose closed her eyes and offered up a prayer that Humphrey knew what vulcanizing meant and that cloud was all the smoke she'd see.

She opened one eye.

Smoke still bloomed from the engine cowling.

The plane lurched forward and then wheeled right. All three engines spun up to half throttle. Their rumble echoed inside the cabin. The plane flexed and creaked over every bump in the field as it picked up speed. The engine kept smoking.

Rose knew she had to tell Rick about the bad seal. She jumped up and headed for the cockpit. Walking through the bouncing cabin felt like trying to ride a bull in a rodeo. She dragged herself forward using seat backs and the plane interior struts for support. She made it to the open cockpit door and stuck her head in on Rick's side.

She didn't need to warn him about the engine. He was staring out the starboard window at the plume of black smoke coming out of the cowling seam. On the instrument panel in front of Rick, a red light flashed over a gauge labeled #3 OIL PRESSURE. The needle on the gauge pointed to zero.

The plane pivoted around on one wheel and pointed the nose into the wind. Humphrey shoved the throttles to wide open. The roar in the cockpit turned deafening and the plane leapt forward.

Out the front windscreen Rose could see the French soldier standing in the field, right in their path. He had his rifle pointed at the plane.

The plane took another hard bounce and nearly threw Rose back into the cabin. She clung onto the edges of the opening to the cockpit with her finger tips. The aircraft gathered more speed and the engine smoke thickened.

Rick grimaced at the oil pressure gauge and then smacked it with his fist. The needle didn't move.

The soldier was now just a dozen yards away. If he fired, he could not miss. If he didn't move, the main engine's prop was going to turn him into ground meat.

Suddenly the engine smoke stopped. The red light in the dash went out and the oil pressure needle swung to the right. Rick and Humphrey pulled back on the steering yokes so hard Rose could see their straining back muscles. The aircraft's nose jerked up.

The soldier flinched and fired. The round went wide. He dove for the ground. The plane seemed to miss him by inches as it climbed. At two thousand feet, Humphrey leveled the plane, rolled back the throttles, and aimed it south for Singapore.

"See," Rick said. "I knew that seal would hold."

Rose punched him in the shoulder. "You big liar. I swear that if we make it back home alive, I'm never setting foot in this plane again."

***

Later that day, Rose sat dozing in one of the passenger seats as the plane flew over the Pacific.

"Miss Rose," Humphrey called back. "We're over the spot on the map you marked."

Rose shook herself wide awake. "Okay. Drop us down to a few hundred feet and head north for a bit."

"Rodger dodger."

Rose crossed the cabin and grabbed the rice sack of artifacts. The plane entered a diving left hand turn. When it leveled out, Rose saw the swells of the Pacific out the window. According to the map and an article she'd once read in National Geographic, beneath the surface was the Mariana Trench. At the turn of the century a Navy ship had recorded that it was over 30,000 feet deep. No better place to hide Rudra's relics.

Rick came back from the cockpit and opened the cabin door. A cold wind blasted into the cabin. Rose dragged the sack over to the opening. She pulled out a jade hand and tossed it out into the sea. A minute later, she sent the second hand to Davy Jones' locker. Then she fished out the Scarlet Heart of Khmer. The sunlight coming in through the door turned it into a dazzling red spectacle.

Rick grabbed Rose's wrist. "Let's not be hasty," he shouted over the wind noise.

Rose looked at her husband. The wind blew his hair in a hundred directions at once and he squinted against it. He still managed a smile.

"We don't have to dump this ruby," he said. "Without the hands, it's harmless. And it's worth a fortune."

"It's polluted by Rudra, infused with her evil spirit. It will call someone to do something bad."

"We're going home broke, Rosie. Look, I know a guy who can recut it into two pieces, maybe more. That ought to knock the bad mojo out of it."

Rose grabbed Rick's wrist where he grabbed hers. "I promised," she shouted. "Do you want to call down the bad karma of me breaking that promise?"

"No." Rick let go of her wrist and looked away. "But I can't watch thousands of dollars drop into the ocean."

Rose flung the ruby out the door. As it dropped it caught the sun from above and the light reflected off the ocean below. It burst into light like a signal flare. Then it splashed into the ocean and disappeared.

Rick closed the door and the cabin went still and silent save the drone of the engines. 'We're officially poor."

"And it feels wonderful."

CHAPTER THIRTY-ONE

One week later

Rick and Rose stood on opposite sides of the counter in their shop. The ledger for the store lay open between them and a stack of bills sat beside it. Rick wasn't much on the business side of the store, but he knew the number in the Current Cash entry did not have enough decimal places to make the stack of bills disappear.

"We'll find a way out of this," Rick said.

Rose shook her head. "I don't see how. Even if we sold all our inventory, it wouldn't cover what we owe."

"I can't help but think I bear some responsibility for this financial mess."

"If by *some* you mean *all*, then you hit the nail on the head."

The door opened and a deliveryman entered with a parcel wrapped in brown paper about a foot long and a half-foot long on the other sides. Rick signed for it and the deliveryman left. Rick checked the address and raised an eyebrow.

"This was shipped from Charya in Phnom Penh," Rick said.

Rose looked wary. "The last thing we got from Cambodia nearly killed us."

"Charya wouldn't send something dangerous. I mean, I don't think he would."

Rick opened the package and pulled out a lacquered vase. A pair of the golden fishes was painted on the body.

"That's beautiful," Rose said.

"And 100% not cursed. I hope."

A note stuck out of the top. Rick pulled out the note and read it aloud.

"Some of the freed men from Chraknorok tracked me down to thank me. Didn't seem right to not share it. Enjoy and never tell me what you did with the things in the rice sack."

"Charya made a lot of effort to send us a vase," Rose said.

Rick looked inside, then turned it upside down. A cloth bag dropped out atop the ledger. He opened it and upended it.

Three small rubies tumbled out.

Rose's eyes lit up. "Wow."

Rick picked one up and held it up to the light. It was uncut. "The escaping laborers must have found some of the discarded rubies from the mines and taken them when they were freed. And Charya was decent enough to cut us in on this reward."

"I'm sure the distribution was less than fifty-fifty."

"That goes without saying, if I know Charya. But these should bring in enough to put us back on our feet and a little bit ahead." Rick beamed. "So, we had an adventure and came out with cash in our pockets. You may thank your husband whenever you have the time."

"My schedule will always be too full to do that."

Rick set the ruby back down by the others. "You know, I'm starting to believe in karma."

***

If there was one thing Rick understood, it was when you had a run of good luck, you needed to ride that current. The delivery of a bag of rubies was one hell of a lucky event, and he wasn't about to let that luck run out without leveraging it.

So that night he attended the weekly poker game run out of a back room at one of the Savannah bars. The players weren't the richest men in the city, but they were second-tier rich. Rick had wrangled an irregular invitation from Doug McAtee, the organizer, after some business deals. He and Rose had sold him a few fine antiques when Doug had been flush, and bought from him at a fair price when he hadn't been. Rick wasn't permitted to be a regular because he had an annoying tendency to win.

Tonight, the fifth man at the table was a newcomer, a young Englishman named Colin Farr. His passenger steamship had stopped overnight in Savannah and after being cooped up at sea for weeks, he'd decided to exploit the opportunity to enjoy time on dry land. And the man had been enjoying it. He'd been drinking before he started to play, and hadn't stopped as the game progressed. By now he was squinting at cards to tell what they were and the chips he tossed into the pot frequently missed the target. His stack of remaining chips was pretty small.

Rick knew better than to mix drinking and wagering. He'd mastered nursing one drink for an entire evening to stay clear-headed. Of course, sometimes he acted tipsy, to disarm the other players, but that was just part of the game. Half of playing poker was what went on beyond the cards in your hand.

Right now, the cards in his hand were good. Three queens and two eights were going to be tough to beat. The three regulars had folded as the price to stay in the hand got steeper. Now it was just down to him and Colin.

Colin had the wan complexion of a man who spent more time in London fog than seaside sunshine. High cheekbones accentuated his sallow cheeks and the part in his dark, unruly hair seemed to be as much combing as it could tolerate. His bleary eyes checked the cards in his hand far too many times for a man with a winning hand.

The bet was to Rick, a ten dollar raise. It looked like Colin was hoping he'd capitulate under the weight of the bet. Colin had hoped wrong.

Rick slid a pile of chips into the pot. "See your ten and raise you twenty."

Rick knew that was all the man had left. Colin looked with distress at the paltry pile of chips at his seat. He slid his remaining chips in, then eyed the chips remaining at Rick's seat.

"I call your twenty," Colin said, "and raise you whatever you have left with this."

He unbuttoned his shirt and removed a gold chain from around his neck. At the end dangled an opal-cut, sapphire pendant so dark blue it was almost black. A golden Egyptian ankh symbol attached it to the chain. Colin held it suspended over the pot.

"This is worth more than what you have there," he said.

Rick gripped the chain between two fingers and held the sapphire up to the light. To the naked eye it seemed flawless. It was also over half an inch long. Even a sapphire half the size was worth more than what Rick had left to bet.

"Now, now," Doug said. The plump banker sat to Rick's left. "Table stakes rules, Mr. Farr. You can't bet more than you had at the table at the start of the hand. All you can do is call Mr. Sinclair's bet."

Rick considered his run of good luck and the price this sapphire would fetch when he sold it. "I'm okay with breaking the rules one time for our guest, if everyone else is."

The others at the table shrugged their indifference. Doug sighed. "Very well."

Colin smiled and dropped the sapphire into the pot. Rick slid in his remaining chips.

Colin grinned and showed his cards. Three jacks and two aces. "How do you like that hand?"

"A lot better than you'll like this one."

Rick laid down his queens and eights. Colin's jaw sagged.

"Should have stuck with table stakes, Mr. Farr," Doug said.

Rick picked up the sapphire from the pot and held it in his hand. The stone felt unbelievably cold. A sense of dread darkened his heart. He dropped the sapphire back onto the chips.

Rick took a deep breath and exhaled. The clock on the wall said it was well-past midnight. He'd been up for too many hours in a row and his mind was playing tricks on him. A rock was a rock.

There couldn't be anything supernatural about this stone.

AFTERWORD

Rick and Rose have survived another adventure, but it looks like more trouble might be right around the corner. You can check out their previous adventures *Quest for the Queen's Temple, Voyage to Blackbeard's Island,* and *Search for the City of Gold* while I piece that new story together.

I like to mix as much real history as I can into the fiction, so let's see what I got away with this time.

The story hinges on some very real history of Cambodia, or as it was called back in the 13th century, the Khmer Empire. Around 1177, King Jayavarman VII decided that the Hindu gods had failed him after a string of military defeats. He abandoned the Hindu religion for Buddhism and forced the entire empire to follow suit. That went as well as most forced religious conversions do. There was chaos and rebellion, though the people and city of Chraknorok in this story are a complete invention.

However, the inspiration for Chraknorok and the monastery guarding the Scarlet Heart ruby came from a real place. Angkor Wat was a vast religious complex in Cambodia, built when Hindu was the state religion. It spanned 400 acres and hosted over a thousand buildings. At one point it also became the seat of secular power. But after invaders sacked it, the king built a new city to replace it. A small number of monks remained on site and Angkor Wat slowly fell into disrepair. European colonizers "rediscovered" it in the mid-1800s. By then, most parts of it had been overgrown and the buildings had collapsed.

Today much of this architectural and cultural treasure has been restored and it is a popular tourist destination. I hope to go see it someday if Rick and Rose can sell enough books to cover the cost.

Rudra the Destroyer was an actual Vedic god. This religion pre-dated Hinduism and it is possible that Rudra was a precursor being to Hindu's Shiva, though I don't treat her as such in this story. Rudra is sometimes called the god of the storms, which is where I got the idea of being able to compress air and use it as a weapon. There are plenty of stories about Rudra and the battles to conquer her if you want to head down that internet rabbit hole. My story of her attempted resurrection isn't part of any of those. Score one for my creativity.

The Buddhist symbols on the talismans Dara gives our heroic couple actually represent what is described in the book. Monks do sometimes reside in monasteries run by abbots. The concepts of reincarnation and karma are part of Buddhist teaching. That's about the end of an accurate depiction of the religion. As far as I know, the hybrid version Dara practices that includes elements of magic is a fabrication.

Poor Humphrey is bested by a troop of nasty monkeys. These primates are modeled after the long-tailed macaque. They live in Cambodia's shrublands, lowland rainforests, and coastal forests. They travel in groups of 20 to 100. They are omnivorous and not above stealing food from human beings. These super-smart monkeys use rocks to bash open shellfish and wash their food before eating. I've never heard of them being possessed by ghosts, but if you have, I'm all ears.

Those spirits in the story reside in an abandoned rubber plantation. Rubber manufacturing took off in the beginning of the 20th century as the need for automobile tires and many other rubber items grew. The tropics were the place to grow it, and colonial powers were quick to start commercial plantations. In most instances this included compelling local people into service on those farms. Their treatment was often horrible and many plantation owners viewed these workers as expendable. On the bright side, commercial rubber production generally failed and these plantations were abandoned. As Rick would say "You know, I'm starting to believe in karma."

In the story, the magic discs and monastery door are made of rosewood. In real life, rosewood doesn't have mystical powers, but it is a beautiful hardwood native to southwest Asia. If you decide to use some in a project or purchase furniture made from it, be sure it is properly sourced. Illegal logging of old growth rosewood has made a mess of many Asian parks and reserves.

Thanks go out to my faithful Beta readers Donna Fitzpatrick, Lucielle Bransfield, and Deb DeAlteriis for catching all my typos, continuity, and general grammar errors. Also thank you Severed Press for making my adventure stories come to life all over the world.

While you await Rick and Rose's next story, you might want to sample a Grant Coleman Adventure. He's a paleontologist who keeps getting roped into expeditions that find supposedly extinct giant creatures. He's no hero, though. He's a little overweight, he's a little clumsy, and he's very sarcastic. He's not happy when these things keep happening to him. Check out his tales here at https://www.russellrjames.com/grant-coleman-adventures/.

You can also try a Ranger Kathy West Adventure. She and Nathan Toland are National Park rangers who find out that some of our parks were secretly created not for our enjoyment, but because something big and dangerous in the middle didn't need to get out. Those are all described at

https://www.russellrjames.com/ranger-kathy-west-adventures/.

Thanks to all of you who have been reading my stories in print or digitally or been listening to the audio versions. It has been great chatting with you online and wonderful to meet you in person at the dozen or so con signings I do each year. You've all made my author dream come true. Check out my con schedule at www.russellrjames.com and you can also sign up for my monthly newsletter there and keep up to date on my writing, garage projects, and con appearances.

Time to start my Egyptian research and see what Rick is about to get them into. I bet it isn't good.

-Russell James

www.ingramcontent.com/pod-product-compliance
Lightning Source LLC
Chambersburg PA
CBHW061231170626
46809CB00007B/2619